QUEEN

SACRIFICE

QUEEN SACRIFICE

RED RAIN #8

RACHEL NEWHOUSE

To Sean
Stay in school.
(That's how you become a genius.)

Stay in church.
(That's how you avoid becoming an *evil* genius.)

JULY 2076

1: PHILADELPHIA

Nic was dead.

I admitted it as soon as the strangers in the subway stopped administering CPR. Two men had been taking turns trying desperately to pump life back into Nic's chest. The first gave three more compressions—then stopped. He held his fingers against Nic's purple neck. Then he sat back on his haunches with an exhausted sigh.

The other man gestured at Nic's body, as if offering to take over. The first shook his head.

That's when I realized Nic hadn't been breathing for at least twenty minutes, maybe more. Where was the ambulance? I could only imagine it was stuck in Beijing's rush hour, trapped in a sea of cars while a man died.

It was too late now. Even if they could bring him back, there would be nothing left. He would be worse off than my dad.

He was gone.

The rest of the world seemed to reboot around that fact. A subway employee peeled the defibrillator pads off Nic's bluish-white chest and wrapped the cords back up in the orange box. One of the men who had administered CPR stood and pulled out his phone to make a call. Vaguely, I registered the screech of a train arriving at the station, and the crowd shifted as hundreds of evening commuters tried to cram themselves on the cars. All around me, people chattered in a language I couldn't understand as rush hour continued unabated.

I couldn't move. I felt stuck in a time loop, only able to repeat the same thought over and over like a glitched electronic as my brain tried and failed, tried and failed to accept what was going on.

He's dead he's dead he's dead.

I stared at Nic's body, sprawled on the dirty platform tile. Even in death, his face had flatlined into that familiar disinterested frown. A few months ago, I had feared that frown. When we'd met, Dr. Nic Von Nieuwenhuyse had been an enemy, a heartless criminal, a creator of superweapons. Now, all I could think was that I wouldn't be alive without him. He had come back to Earth from Mars to stop me from making the biggest mistake of my life. He'd saved me.

And now I was the reason he was dead.

I looked down at my right hand. I'd killed Nic. The chip in my palm had given him an electromagnetic shock and sent him into cardiac arrest when I'd grabbed his hand. The chip had been designed as an assassination weapon, intended for General Secretary Mong, the leader of the United. The weapon should have killed my greatest enemy. Instead, it killed the closest thing I had to family, at least on this planet.

My brain suddenly restarted as a torrent of guilt knocked loose a whirlwind of unanswered questions. *How, how did this happen?* My chip should have been coded for the General Secretary's DNA. Did it malfunction? It hadn't shocked anyone else, and I'd had it in my hand for a week. Why now? Why Nic? *Why is this happening—*

I involuntarily shrieked when someone touched my arm. I looked up to see a paramedic gently pushing me aside. I saw her uniform and bag of supplies and instantly grabbed onto a false sense of hope. I gripped Nic's shoulder. "Please, you have to help him!" I screamed. "Surely there's something—"

One of the men who had administered CPR spoke over me in Mandarin, pointing at Nic's body and then at the defibrillator. The paramedic knelt next to Nic and checked for a pulse in three different places, then pulled a stethoscope out of her bag and listened to his heart. Lastly, she pulled out a light, pried one of Nic's eyes open, and tested his unblinking pupils.

All of this happened in the space of less than a minute, but for me, it felt like an eternity. Each thing she checked was like a nail in Nic's coffin, each failed test another screaming reminder that he wasn't coming back. This was really happening. Nic was really dead. Nic was dead, and I was alone, and I had nowhere to go, and it was all my fault…

The paramedic closed Nic's eye, then turned to her partner and dictated something. He nodded and typed on his tablet.

I knew even without being able to speak the language what they were saying, but some unhelpful stranger behind me translated. "They're declaring him dead on the scene."

"No," I whimpered, desperate for this all to be a cruel nightmare, but no one even heard me. *God, why why why? What did I do wrong?*

The male paramedic bent over and grabbed Nic's limp hand. He pressed Nic's thumb to his tablet. Instantly, the device screeched and flashed red. I saw a glimpse of the warning on the screen, written in both Mandarin and English:

NATIONAL SECURITY RISK. DETAIN AT ALL COSTS.

I laughed, a deranged howl that quickly melted into a wail of anguish. Even dead, Nic was still a wanted criminal. And it was all because of me.

I wanted to throw myself on his body and beg and plead for forgiveness—from him, God, anyone. I wanted to recant every choice I'd made for the last six weeks and undo all my actions. All the mistakes, all the times I'd refused to take Nic's advice, all the failures that had brought us to this point, to Nic lying dead on the floor of a Beijing subway station. I would do anything, say anything, take any punishment—if it would just bring Nic back.

"God, I'm sorry!" I shrieked aloud, not caring who heard me. "Please don't do this! I need him!" I shook Nic's shoulder violently, causing his head to roll.

I heard the squeak of wheels on tile and saw them push a stretcher up to us. The female paramedic turned to me. Murmuring something that was probably "excuse me," she gently grasped my arms and pried my hands off Nic's body.

As soon as my fingers left his shoulder, it hit me.

This isn't right.

I snapped back to attention as that revelation filled me with pulsing anger. This *wasn't* right. Nic shouldn't be dead. Less than a half hour ago, he'd told me that he'd seen a vision about my future. He knew we were supposed to be in Beijing—us, together—because I was supposed to lead the revolution and he was supposed to help me. That was the whole reason we were here. That was the whole reason God had brought us together. God had called us. Not just me—*us.*

And God doesn't lie.

"This isn't right," I whispered. I sat up on my knees. "This isn't right!" I repeated, louder, for myself and all the spirits that were listening. "You can't have him!"

The paramedic tried to pull me back, but I shoved her aside. I leaned over Nic and planted my palms flat on his heart. I looked straight into his face and declared loudly and clearly as if he could hear me: "You aren't supposed to die. You're supposed to help me. You're supposed to be here, in Beijing. This is what you're called to do. This is your purpose. God chose you!"

A murmur rippled up the crowd, although whether it was because I'd yelled the name of an illegal religious figure or because I was making a scene on a dead man's chest, I'll never know. I stared at Nic's closed eyes as the Holy Spirit welled up in my throat with an indescribable pressure. There were a million thoughts swirling around in my soul, but there was only one thing I knew for sure. I screamed it out and hoped all the powers of hell heard me:

"This isn't right, and in the name of Jesus, you are going to live!"

I shoved down on Nic's chest with all my weight—and he yelled.

He jerked upright, knocking me backwards. He whipped around, arms flinging like a ragdoll, as he scanned the crowd with rabid eyes. The bystanders shrieked and pulled back; even the paramedics leaned away like they were afraid to touch him. He panted and started sweating profusely as his head jerked back and forth.

And then he spotted me.

Suddenly, he seemed to repossess his body. He blinked, and his vision focused on me, gaze clear. "Philadelphia?"

I burst into relieved tears. "Nic! Oh God, thank you! You brought him back!"

My words gave Nic pause. He looked down at his ripped shirt, then at over at the defibrillator box, then up at the paramedics. "What just happened?"

He added a couple of extra words—one of which I knew I shouldn't repeat—and that's when I knew he'd be all right.

"My—my chip." I struggled to explain as all the leftover adrenaline made my voice shaky. "It—I—killed you. You were dead. You weren't breathing for like twenty minutes."

He looked down at my right hand, then back up at my face. "Then why am I still here?"

I met his gaze. "I-I prayed for you. God brought you back from the dead."

We stared at each other, and in that flicker of understanding, I knew he realized exactly what had happened. He knew what God had done for him—for me.

Nic opened his mouth, but just then, the paramedics decided to come back to work. The female grabbed his arm and tried to lay him back down. The male leaned over and asked him a question. Nic ignored it, instead staring at the tablet in the man's hand.

The red warning was still displayed on the screen. And that's when I remembered: Nic's file was marked with the highest security warning there was. As soon as he checked into the hospital, they would arrest him. And then Asia, his ex-girlfriend and a top United official, would do whatever she wanted with him.

And I doubted it would be pleasant.

I scrambled up, adjusting my backpack. "We need to go!"

Nic struggled to copy me, but he barely made it to his feet. He stumbled, nearly crashing into the paramedic, and grabbed the back of his head. I could see his blond hair was soiled with blood from where he'd cracked his head on the tile.

Both paramedics grabbed his arms. "Please, sir," the male one clipped in poor English, "you need to go to the hospital."

Nic weakly brushed them off. "I'm fine, I'm fine," he insisted.

One of the civilians who had administered CPR joined the chase. "Sir, you really need to get checked out."

I grabbed Nic's sleeve and tried to pull him away. "He'll be fine, I promise." I turned and scanned the clogged platform, looking for a way out. Maybe if we could make a break for it, we could lose them in the crowd.

The paramedics were having none of it. The male one tried to shove Nic onto the stretcher, even though he was barely half Nic's height. Nic jerked back from him and almost lost his balance. The subway employee whipped out his radio and shouted into it, and whatever he said did not sound encouraging. I knew we had to get out of here *right now*, or we'd cause a bigger scene.

I pinched Nic's elbow. "Nic!" I hissed. "Your gun!"

He lifted his jacket and reached for his holstered weapon, then hesitated. The entire crowd sucked in its breath. The paramedics froze, as if waiting to see what he'd do. Nic scanned the throng of civilians around us—then grabbed his gun and threw it on the floor.

The crowd scattered away from it, shouting. "Nic!" I screeched.

He whipped to face me. "Run. Get out of here!"

I forgot to breathe as I struggled to process what he was telling me. "But Nic, I—"

"I'm not getting out of this," he said, words rapid but calm. "I can't run in this condition. Get out of here, go back to the Tangs."

"I'm not leaving you!" I cried. *Not after you just died!*

"Phil, listen to me." He grabbed my shoulders. "It's not me Asia wants—it's you."

"But why—"

He spoke over me. "No matter what happens to me, no matter what you hear, I need you to promise that you won't come for me. Do you understand?"

I didn't, not at all. "Nic, I—"

He shook my shoulders so hard my neck hurt. "Promise me!"

I didn't have a chance to respond. I heard the shriek of a whistle and shouts of "*Jingcha!* Police!" I saw commotion in my peripheral; the crowd rippled like a predator was breaking through the waves on a lake.

Nic saw it too. His eyes scanned the crowd for an escape— and just then the horn of an approaching train echoed down the tunnel. I felt the swell in the crowd and saw several subway employees trying to shepherd gawking bystanders away as the queue flowed towards the edge of the platform.

Nic looked back into my face. His gray eyes were stern but unafraid as he repeated, "Don't *ever* come back."

And then he grasped my shoulders and pushed me away from him.

I stumbled backwards with a yell—just as the train arrived in the station. The crowd surged forward with one accord, crushing me from all sides. I grabbed the arm of the person nearest to me, knowing that if I fell, I'd be trampled. He grunted something and shrugged me off.

I crashed into the person behind us, who elbowed me forward. I struggled to stay on my feet as I twisted around, looking for Nic, but I couldn't see him or the paramedics anywhere. All I could see was a tightly packed mob of jackets and backpacks as a sea of unfamiliar faces funneled me towards the subway.

"No, please, I don't want to get on! Excuse me! Please!" I shoved the person nearest to me aside, but as soon as I created a gap, three more people crammed in to fill the space. No one was listening to me as a garbled announcement blared over the intercom.

I felt myself being carried along like a stick in a river as the congested crowd crammed onto the car. The throng seemed to pack itself tighter and tighter, as if someone was sucking all the air out of the station. Bodies pressed in around me like a noose cinching until I couldn't even move my arms.

No, God, this can't be happening! Get me out of here! Nic!

No one budged. Elbows and knees prodded me forward, while white-gloved subway employees literally shoved people onto the car. I tripped over the gap from the platform to the train and almost knocked the person in front of me over. The queue continued to carry me into the center of the car; I couldn't even see out the windows around the sea of commuters. I blindly groped for the handlebar and managed to grab it just as the train lurched away from the station.

The motion sent my heart plummeting to my stomach. It was too late. Even if I could get off, Nic would be long gone. They'd take him to the hospital, and then Asia would send him to prison—or worse. It was over.

I was alone.

2: PHILADELPHIA

I rode the train to the end of the line.

I didn't have much of a choice; the rush-hour crowd was so thick that I probably couldn't have gotten off had I wanted to. I stood in the middle of the car, gripping the handlebar with both hands. It was the only thing holding me up. My system was still reeling from the sleep medication I'd taken earlier in the day; that, combined with the throb of unspent emotions, was making the world spin erratically like a washing machine that had gotten knocked off balance. The jerking motion of the train didn't help. I clenched my jaw and took shallow breaths through my nose, afraid that if I opened my mouth, I might scream or vomit or worse.

Eventually, the ebb and flow of commuters began to wane. As soon as a seat on the wall freed up, I sank into it. I leaned my head against the window and watched the lights in the tunnel flicker in and out of focus as the train passed an endless number of platforms. Stop and go, in and out, dark and light flashing back and forth, until finally the darkness won.

I jerked awake when a well-meaning passenger shook my shoulder. I sat upright with a gasp, startling her and everyone else in the car. I looked around at their confused faces and tried to remember where I was. How long had I been out? *That stupid medication must have finally gotten the better of me.*

The woman leaned over me and spoke kindly in Mandarin.

"I'm fine," I said, hoping my inflection would overcome the language barrier. I faked a smile and stood up, shouldering my backpack. She didn't look convinced, but she nodded and backed away.

Holding onto the handlebar, I inched over to the door. As soon as the train stopped at the next station, I shoved through the dwindling crowd and ran for the stairs.

I emerged into the warm night. Rush hour traffic had died off, but Beijing's nightlife was more than picking up the slack. Every storefront was lit with a blinding array of spotlights and red neon characters. Lanterns were strung across the road, casting an artificial red-orange glow on everything and making the whole block look like it was on fire. The dinner crowd clogged the street as families crammed around sidewalk tables and college students formed laughing queues in front of order counters. The air thrummed with chatter and the sizzle of woks.

The vendor nearest to the subway entrance—a kindly-looking grandpa manning a cart—called out to me, but I ducked my head and kept walking. I had to find someplace out of sight. I hurried down the block, dodging pedestrians, and ducked into an alley. I emerged onto the next street and found myself on the edge of the river.

Breathing a sigh of relief, I crossed the walking bridge to the other side and ran along the bank until I found an empty dock. The building behind it was either abandoned or closed for the night, and no one was in sight. Further downstream, I heard families gathering on their waterfront verandas, but the night had grown dark enough that I doubted they could see me.

Shrugging off my backpack, I sank onto the mossy brick. I took deep breaths through my nose and willed my heart to slow. Leaning back against the building behind me, I closed my eyes and waited for my thoughts to settle.

They didn't. If anything, they churned faster in the silence. *What am I going to do?*

Nic wasn't coming back—I knew that. As soon as he got out of the hospital, Asia would put him in jail, and then what? I knew she still had eyes for him, but he'd rather die than give her the time of day after all she'd done to us, never mind to his parents. Besides, Nic claimed it wasn't him Asia wanted; it was me.

What did she want with me? I replayed our interactions over the past week and easily came up with the answer: She wanted me to kill her father.

Asia was General Secretary Mong's daughter, and evidently, she had her sights set on his throne. According to Nic, she'd known about the chip in my palm. She'd been aware of the assassination plot and done everything in her power to make sure it succeeded. She'd pretended to be my friend, adopted me into her inner circle, and groomed me until I looked like a porcelain doll. She'd spared no expense to turn me into a polite high society girl, all so that when the time came for me to meet her father at that dreadful state dinner, he'd want to shake my hand.

It had almost worked. The General Secretary had been delighted to meet me and offered me his friendship—but at the last minute, I'd listened to the Holy Spirit and refused. I'd bowed instead of shaking the General's hand. He'd taken it as a show of humility and been none the wiser. He'd even accepted my invitation to host him for dinner.

Asia, however, had been less thrilled by the turn of events. She'd ambushed Nic and me outside of the party and tried to blackmail Nic into turning himself in. He had not obliged, and we'd spent the last few days running across Beijing, struggling to stay off the grid while looking for a way back to Mars. It had been an exhausting game of cat and mouse.

And now Asia had won.

I slapped my hands over my face as a few hot tears escaped. What would she do to Nic? If it was me she wanted, then she wouldn't be kind to him. Would she torture him? Make him stand trial for his crimes? He was guilty of many—and there was no such thing as a fair trial in the United.

I tried to formulate a prayer, but it jammed in my throat. What was I even supposed to pray for? Asia had the first move. I knew she wouldn't kill Nic—at least not right away—not if she wanted to coerce me into coming home. He wasn't safe, but he had time. Until then, I had no choice but to wait and see what Asia would do.

But where was I supposed to go in the meantime? I had to stay off the grid. I had multiple identities, and all of them were dangerous. Philadelphia Smyrna, my birth name, was wanted for being "Blue Fire," the figurehead of a revolution. Andromeda Nolan, my adopted name, was clean as far as the government was concerned, but I knew Asia was watching my file closely. If I made any electronic activity under either name, Asia would know exactly where I was—if the police didn't get to me first.

I had to hide. Nic had said to go back to the Tangs, but I couldn't go back there, not after what I did to them.

I winced as the events of earlier today rolled through me. The Tangs were old friends of the Vons and leaders in the Chinese underground. They'd taken Nic and me in and introduced us to Jael, a powerful tech mogul with the ability to get us off the grid.

The only problem was that we'd found out she'd been controlling our lives for the past several months. When we'd met with her earlier this afternoon, she'd informed us that she was responsible for creating "Blue Fire." She was the one who had made my videos trend, manipulating the algorithm to build a freedom movement around my name.

All this time, I'd believed God was responsible for creating Blue Fire. I thought it—I—was a miracle. Turns out, one woman had been pulling the strings and using my image to start a war— and she'd never even bothered to introduce herself.

I'd felt so enraged and betrayed that I'd *shot* her. I'd grabbed Nic's gun off the table and hit her straight in the chest. The weapon had been set on stun—hopefully—but I'd also threatened to turn the Tangs' underground church over to the government and stolen a motorbike. I'd been reeling from an overdose of sleep medication, sure, but that only accounted for some of my actions. The real reason I'd snapped was that I was sick and tired of being everyone's puppet and was determined not to let anyone use me ever again.

I couldn't go back to the Tangs after that. What was I going to do, waltz into their house and say, *"My bad, I will be your Blue Fire"*? They'd never believe me about Nic's vision, and even if they did, they wouldn't trust me after what I'd done. *I* wouldn't trust me. I'd proven I was an emotionally unstable teenager who shattered under pressure, and that was the truth.

I pulled my legs in and pressed my face to my knees. I couldn't go back to the Tangs, but I also couldn't stay out here. I couldn't go online; if I bought food or made any purchase, Asia would trace the activity. And I had other enemies in Beijing. Jayde, my former ally, was no doubt still in the city. *If he catches me...*

I shuddered and tried to block out the nightmares of Jayde's cruelty. *What do I do, God?* I mentally screamed, struggling to push a prayer past the whirlwind of fear and hopelessness. *I need Your wisdom. Where do I go?*

For an answer, something furry brushed my arm.

I shrieked and scrambled back. I looked down to see a scrawny gray cat rubbing around my legs.

"Tommy?" I gasped in disbelief.

He mewed and climbed in my lap. I scooped him up and pressed him to my chest, squeezing him to make sure he was real. I never thought I'd see my cat again. Calling him "mine" was perhaps being overly optimistic; Tommy was a stray that Nic and I had picked up a few days ago, but he'd seemed content to follow us. I'd left him at the Tangs' earlier this afternoon, and I thought that would be the last I'd hear of him.

I held him up and stared into his yellow eyes. "How did you get here?"

As if on cue, footsteps pounded down the alley, and someone yelled my name. "Philli!"

I jumped up, gripping Tommy in my arms. I turned to see my friends John and Dowe racing towards me, the beam from their flashlight bouncing on the brick.

"It's her!" John shouted, as if Dowe weren't right behind him. "Good dog, Tommy!"

"He's not a dog." Dowe smacked his partner upside the head. "Dogs go *woof,* and Tommy goes... not that."

"Yeah, well, he can track like a dog, so he gets good boy treats."

"I can respect that."

They reached me and crashed to a stop. I took a step back. John and Dowe had been in the room when I shot Jael; they knew what I'd done.

If John sensed my hesitation, he wasn't deterred by it—not that either of them made a habit of paying attention to social cues. He stepped forward and opened his arms. "Philadelphia, we were so worried."

I took the invitation. I set Tommy down and threw myself into John's arms. He caught me and wrapped me in a fatherly embrace. The affection broke down the dam of guilt and shame inside of me, and I gripped his shirt and burst into tears. "I'm so sorry," I squeaked out in between sobs. "I'm so sorry!"

He shushed me. "We know you are. We know when our girl isn't acting like herself."

Dowe rubbed my shoulder. "Yeah, just next time you get lost, remember the rule: Sit down and wait for help to arrive. We've been tracking you for *two hours*, waiting for you to stop moving."

"Wait." I pulled away from John. "How did you find me?" My phone wasn't turned on; they should have had no way to track me.

Dowe pointed at my backpack. "Your tablet. It's online."

I grabbed my backpack off the ground and unzipped it. They were right; the tablet I'd borrowed from the Tangs was turned on. But how? I'd powered it off last time I used it.

I gripped my bag as realization rolled through me. Nic must have turned it on. He must have grabbed my backpack before we went in the subway station and brought the device online when I wasn't looking. The tablet wasn't registered to me, so Asia couldn't track it, but the Tangs could.

I pushed tears away with the heel of my hand. Yet again, Nic had protected me. He'd been thinking ahead and made sure help would be able to find me, even while I was having a mental breakdown and brandishing a loaded gun.

"Let's go," John urged. He scooped my cat up, and Tommy willingly settled on his shoulder. "If we hurry, there might be some dinner left. Where's Nic?"

A sob ripped out of me involuntarily, which probably told them everything they needed to know.

"Oh no," Dowe murmured. "Philli, what happened?"

"My chip, it… he was…" I winced and skipped to the relevant information. "They arrested him."

There was silence, but only for a fraction of a second. "Well, no time to waste, then. We all know how terrible Nic looks in prison orange." Dowe gestured and started walking. "Jael will know what to do."

They turned and led the way down the dock. I didn't follow. "John, Dowe, I… I can't go back there. Jael won't help me."

Dowe glanced back and used every muscle in his face to make an incredulous look. "Why not?" he exclaimed, as if that was the stupidest thing I'd ever said.

"You were there!" I threw my hands up. "I… I shot her."

John shrugged. "Yeah? And it was a real good shot, too."

I gaped at him.

Dowe grinned. "I promise, it's not the first time our boss has been shot."

"And if it's the last, she's doing something wrong," John added. "Come on, let's go!" They took off down the alley, taking my cat with them.

I relented, throwing my backpack on my shoulders and racing to keep up. I doubted Jael would be as nonchalant about the ordeal as John and Dowe, but I knew providence when I saw it. I'd asked God where He wanted me to go, and He'd sent John and Dowe—it couldn't get more obvious than that.

I followed them around the corner, where their motorbikes were parked. Tommy seemed content to stay with John, so I rode with Dowe. We followed the river south to the Tangs' neighborhood. I watched as the glare and neon of the commercial district faded away to reveal the stained white stone of the traditional two-story homes that crammed along the canal. I saw factory smokestacks piercing the horizon, faintly backlit by the light pollution of the inner city, and knew we were close.

John and Dowe slowed as we entered an affluent district of courtyard homes. We drove under a small stone arch into a brick pavilion, and there was the Tangs' house. The family was all gathered on the wooden veranda that overlooked the river, sitting around the long table that contained the remnants of dinner. There were shouts and exclamations as we rode into the courtyard, and Lanzhou and his cousin Bowen ran towards us.

I swallowed a flash of shame as I climbed off the motorbike. I knew custom would have me address Lanzhou's father, the senior Tang, first, but Lanzhou was the one I had wronged the most. It was his bike I stole, after all.

I met him on the edge of the veranda and bowed as low as I could. "I'm so sorry," I declared, struggling to keep the tears out of my voice. "Please forgive me. I think I know where your bike is, and if not, I'll replace it."

He gripped my shoulder. "I'm not worried about the bike. I'm worried about you."

I looked up into his gentle smile. "I promise, it won't happen again. I just…" I struggled to explain my behavior, but there was no explanation for it. So, I settled for the truth. "I panicked."

"I know," he reassured me, "and I'm sorry for putting you in that situation. Will you forgive me?"

I frowned at him. He was apologizing to *me*? He'd done nothing wrong.

He kneaded my shoulder. "I didn't realize the doctor had given you sleep medication. If I had, I would have insisted you stay home and rest. I never should have let you go to that meeting."

"But it was my choice," I argued. Even Nic had tried to get me to go back to bed, but I'd refused.

"I know, and what you did was incredibly foolish," Lanzhou admitted. "But I'm the adult *and* your host. It would be dishonor on me if I didn't recognize that I'd set you up to fail. Will you forgive me and my family?"

I stared at him. I was so used to taking all the blame—to everyone always telling me that everything was my fault—that I didn't know what to do when someone else accepted responsibility. The relief and forgiveness welled up inside my chest so much it hurt. I had no idea what to say, so I hugged him instead. I grabbed him around the waist and resumed sobbing uncontrollably.

He hesitated, then gingerly reached down and patted my shoulder. "You're forgiven, Philadelphia. And you'll always be a part of this family."

Bowen tapped my arm. "Come, sit down, eat something."

I released Lanzhou and allowed Bowen to guide me to a seat at the table. No sooner had I sat down than Mrs. Tang placed a steaming bowl of rice and sauteed vegetables in front of me. I inhaled several lungfuls of the spicy aroma, letting the zest of ginger and garlic ground my nerves.

John and Dowe took up places at the opposite end of the table. John set Tommy on the floor and immediately began feeding him table scraps. *No wonder they're friends*, I thought with a small smile.

Bowen sat down across from me and leaned on the table. "Tell us what happened," he urged. "Nic…?"

I winced. "He's… he's…" I struggled to find the facts under the clutter of emotions.

Lanzhou tried to help. "There's a death pronouncement on his file," he said, sliding onto the bench next to me, "immediately followed by a location ping checking him into a hospital, where he's apparently very much alive. What's going on?"

"It was my chip." I took a deep breath and held my hand out. "I grabbed his hand, and it sent him into cardiac arrest. He stopped breathing, and they spent at least twenty minutes trying to revive him before they finally gave up."

A murmur rippled around the table. "So, he really was dead," Bowen whispered, as if he was afraid to admit it.

I shuddered, remembering how Nic's face and neck had turned purple. "The paramedics pronounced him dead when they arrived."

The words brought all the grief and terror crashing back down on me. *He was really dead*, I repeated to myself. *Nic died.*

"But?" Lanzhou prodded.

"But..." I stretched the word out, struggling to wrap my mind around the miracle I'd seen with my own two eyes. "God brought him back."

"What do you mean?" Bowen exclaimed.

"God brought him back." I sat up straight and raised my voice. I knew what I saw; Nic's resurrection was a miracle, and I was not going to be shy about it. "I knew it wasn't right—I knew he wasn't supposed to die. So, I prayed, and... he came back to life. Just like that. He sat up and started talking like nothing had happened."

I glanced around the table at the others, desperate for them to believe me. Thankfully, they did.

"Amen!" John and Dowe shouted. Several other family members echoed them in Mandarin. Lanzhou pinched his eyes shut and muttered in tongues, and the senior Mr. Tang raised both his hands.

I wanted to join them, but suddenly, I couldn't breathe. My mind was spinning, but not from fear. I'd seen a dead man brought back to life. I knew God was capable of it; I'd read about it in the Bible, even heard a few stories of it happening to other people. But now I'd *seen* it. God had brought Nic back to life.

Because *I'd* prayed.

Lanzhou's voice yanked me out of my thoughts. "But they still admitted him to the hospital?"

I slumped back in my seat as the rest of the day's events caught up to me. "They'd already called the police. Nic made me leave without him. He told me to come find you."

"And I'm glad you did," Mr. Tang said from his place at the head of the table. "We'll meet with Jael in the morning. She'll know what to do."

I wished I could share his enthusiasm. "I don't think there's anything she can do."

"It's not the first time she's broken someone out of jail," Lanzhou consoled me.

I shook my head. "It's not like that. Asia—Councilwoman Mong—is the one who flagged his file. She'll have him locked down under the highest security."

Bowen and Lanzhou shared a glance. "How do you know the councilwoman?" Lanzhou asked hesitantly.

"She's been hunting us this entire time." I looked up at him and admitted the disgusting truth. "She knew about my chip. She wanted me to kill her father."

"Well, that piece of information would have been good to know sooner," Bowen muttered.

I flushed. I'd never intended to involve the Tangs in the failed assassination plot or my feud with Asia, but it was too late for that now.

"We'll figure it out," Lanzhou insisted, but it sounded like a platitude. "In the meantime, we need to get your chip removed before anyone else gets hurt."

"We know a gal!" John and Dowe crowed in their creepy unison. "She's a wizard with all kinds of implants. She's got a great track record—she's been tuning us up for years."

Lanzhou arched an eyebrow. "I don't know if that constitutes as a great track record…"

I had to admit he was right. John and Dowe looked and acted like a failed cloning experiment; if they'd had any work done, it wasn't functioning within normal parameters. Nevertheless, I would trust a friend of John and Dowe's over some stranger from the underground.

"How soon can she get me in?" I asked.

"If I say 'please,' she'll fit you in tomorrow. I'll make the call." John grinned at me and got up from the table.

"Until then…" Lanzhou tapped my elbow. "Maybe don't hug anybody else. We don't want your chip to malfunction again."

I winced and nodded. I looked down at my palm and once again wondered: *Why now?* I'd touched hundreds of people since getting my chip implanted. I'd met dozens of Asia's friends and shaken hands with countless elites at the party. I'd had contact with clerks and strangers in the subway. And when I'd visited the Tangs' church yesterday, everyone had wanted to shake my hand. Not a single one of them had gotten hurt.

So why now? Why had my chip chosen that very moment to malfunction? What had I done differently?

I pinched my hand as the implication hit me, cold and bitter. Maybe my chip *didn't* malfunction.

Maybe someone was trying to kill Nic.

3: PHILADELPHIA

I kept my theory to myself as I quickly ate the food Mrs. Tang put in front of me. If I was correct, that meant Nic—and I—had more enemies than I realized. It meant there were several people in the Boston underground I couldn't trust, and my friends back home could be in grave danger. Those were steep accusations, and I needed more evidence.

Thankfully, I knew exactly who could help me find the truth.

"May I keep this? There's someone I need to call." I pulled the tablet out of my backpack and showed it to Lanzhou. I figured after I'd stolen a bike, I should at least ask before using their electronics.

"Of course," he said as he started gathering empty dishes off the table. "All your things are still in your room upstairs."

I shuddered as the memory of last night's horrors washed over me. I couldn't sleep in that room; I'd been *kidnapped* from that room. I knew the Tangs were taking precautions, and Jael was keeping a close eye on Jayde. If he checked in anywhere near the Tangs' house, her men would get there first. But those facts weren't enough to override the thick sense of dread that soaked my nerves like lighter fluid. All I could think about was the terror of being held down by strong arms and the pain of being stabbed with a loaded syringe.

I couldn't go back in that room. That was how this whole mess had started; I'd refused to lie down and rest earlier today because I didn't want to be alone up there.

"I don't want to make things difficult, but…" I looked up into Lanzhou's face and searched for understanding. "I can't stay in that room."

He smiled, but the gesture was too sad to bring me any comfort. "How about the room at the end of the hall?"

That was the room Nic had been staying in, which would either help or make me feel more alone. But I would much rather be at the end of the hallway. I nodded.

"And until we get this sorted out, my wife and I will sleep in the room at the top of the stairs. Will that help?" Lanzhou offered.

I wanted to tell him that he didn't have to do that, but it would have been a lie. "Thank you," I said.

He squeezed my shoulder reassuringly.

As soon as I finished my dinner, I grabbed my backpack and hurried upstairs. Tommy followed, mewing as he ran. I rushed past the first bedroom, refusing to look inside, and darted to the room at the end of the hall. I shut and locked the door behind me, then double- and triple-checked to make sure the windows were latched. I knew I was being paranoid, but I wasn't taking any chances.

Turning on the bedside lamp, I gasped when I saw Nic's backpack sitting on the floor. I'd made us leave in such a hurry earlier this afternoon that he hadn't taken it with him. I knew there was nothing of value in there—just a laptop I couldn't bring online and the leftover survival supplies from our race across Beijing—but I was still glad to have something of his.

I kicked off my borrowed house shoes and sank onto the wooden shelf bed. Tommy leapt up beside me, the silk comforter rustling under his paws, and settled by my pillow. I scratched him behind the ears, managing a small smile. He wasn't much of a guard dog, but his furry presence still helped.

Pulling the tablet out of my backpack, I opened the messaging app and was assaulted with a tsunami of notifications. I winced. I knew without looking who the sender was: Stanyard, my boyfriend from back home in Boston. Clearly, he had realized something was wrong; every time I did something stupid, he spammed me with worried messages until I responded.

I opened the chat and reached for the call button, then caught myself. As much as I wanted to see my boyfriend's face, I owed it to someone else to call them first.

I switched to another tab and dialed my brother.

The call rang out the first time. I tried again and prayed his device wasn't on silent. I had no idea what the time conversion between Beijing and the science station on Mars was; would he even be awake?

Mercifully, the call picked up on the third ring. "Philli!"

I hesitated; the voice was feminine and not the one I was expecting. "Cea?" I guessed.

"That's me," she intoned. Her video connected, revealing her face. Cea was Nic's sister, and she was in every way a sprightlier version of him. She had wild blonde curls and freckled cheeks, and she was quick on the draw with both her words and her gun. It was as if God had taken all of Nic's personality and crammed it into a shorter frame.

"It's so good to see you," I said, and realized it was true. It had been over a month since Cea had gone back to Mars, and I'd been so busy starting a revolution and attempting to assassinate a man that we'd barely talked.

"I was just about to say the same thing." She tipped her head to the side and studied me. "I thought you were never going to call—was beginning to think you were mad at me."

I snorted. "For what?"

She arched an eyebrow and held up her left hand, which was adorned with a sparkly wedding ring.

"Oh," I mumbled as the requisite emotions came rushing back. "You mean the part where you and my brother got married *without telling me?*"

Cea and my brother had eloped on a whim a few days ago. Not only had they not told me they were thinking of getting married, but I also had to hear the news from Nic, which was the ultimate insult.

Cea deferred with a bow of her head. "I know, I know, it was a little impulsive. In my defense, I wasn't expecting him to propose right then."

My brother's voice echoed from off-screen. "Yeah, but you're the one who suggested we get married *immediately*. Don't forget that crucial detail."

I caught myself smiling as my older brother came into view. He sat down next to his wife and leaned over so they were both in the frame. I searched his familiar brown eyes and instantly felt safer. "Ephesus," I sighed.

"Philli," he returned warmly, voice full of relief. "I was so worried about you. And... I'm sorry you got left out of the proceedings. But it really is all Cea's fault."

"What?" she squawked and jerked away.

He wrapped one arm around her and pulled her back in. "Don't let this woman lie to you. She's the real instigator."

"You're the one who said yes," I challenged.

His eyes sparkled with delight. "I'm not one to waste an opportunity." He looked down at Cea, and they shared a smile that told me neither of them regretted anything.

"I guess I can forgive you," I said with a dramatic huff. It was hard to stay mad when they were both clearly so happy. Besides, I wasn't one to talk; I hadn't involved Ephesus in any of my plans, and none of them had happy endings.

Cea was the first to return to business. "But what about you, Phil? You gave us all a heart attack."

I cringed; it was a cruelly ironic choice of words. "I know, I'm sorry," I said, but the confession felt cheap even to my ears.

"I'm just glad Nic got there in time," Ephesus said. He forced a smile, but I could clearly read the expression in his eyes: pain, worry, disappointment.

Cea squeezed his knee and started to rise. "I'll let you two talk."

"No, stay, please," I urged. "There's something I need to tell you, and you both need to hear it."

I took a deep breath and walked them through the events of the past twenty-four hours: about Jayde, the meeting with Jael, my breakdown, and Nic's death and arrest. Cea, ever in control, managed to keep it together better than Ephesus did; he interrupted me several times with exclamations and demands for more details. Twice he got up and walked off-camera to vent his emotions.

"I never should have let you stay on Earth," he muttered for perhaps the fifth time after I'd finally finished the story. He raked both hands through his hair and paced behind Cea's seat.

She glanced back at him, then turned to face me. "You're sure Nic is fine?" It was the first question she'd asked since I'd started talking, and I could hear in her inflection the familial love she and Nic were so good at hiding.

"I promise," I insisted. "He remembered everything, and he was talking clearly in whole sentences. He even swore."

She managed a chuckle, but the laugh didn't make it to her eyes. "And you're sure he stopped breathing? He should have at least had some brain damage after that."

I met her gaze. "They gave up administering CPR, Cea. He was dead."

Her eyes wandered. "I guess I just don't understand how that's possible."

I chewed my lip. How was I supposed to explain it? There was nothing to explain. It was God.

Cea changed the subject before I could start preaching. "Why do you think your chip malfunctioned? You haven't had any other issues with it, have you?"

"No, and… that's actually the main reason I'm calling." I sat up straight. "I don't think it was a malfunction."

"Unfortunately, I think you're right." Ephesus came back into frame and returned to his chair. He touched Cea's knee. "Remember when we looked up the logs and saw that someone had accessed Nic's DNA?"

She sucked in her breath and washed white.

"What?" I exclaimed.

He looked at the camera. "We thought someone had broken into Nic's office, so we pulled up the logs. According to the timestamps, someone accessed and modified his DNA file a little over a week ago."

The timing checked out, and it made perfect sense. The doors on the science station were controlled by an experimental system that read DNA through the user's fingertips, which meant the code for Nic's DNA was on file on the servers. What's more, almost everyone who had been associated with me would know that. Jayde even had remote access to the door lock software; he and Stanyard had used it to help me escape when Nic and I had been trapped in Wing 74. Jayde could have easily logged into the station's server and downloaded the code for Nic's DNA.

I skipped my next breath when I realized I was right. Someone wanted Nic dead.

And I knew exactly who that person was.

"Jayde," I snarled, all my anger and distrust coming out in one corrupted syllable. Jayde was the leader of the Boston underground, and he had been the mastermind behind the assassination plot. The entire operation had been his idea. Surely, he was the one who had plotted Nic's death.

Ephesus wasn't so easily convinced. "But why would he want Nic dead?"

I didn't have an answer for that. Jayde and Nic barely knew each other. But Jayde was violent and impulsive; he needed very little incentive for murder.

"And why would he use you?" Cea pressed. "You and Nic weren't even on the same planet. Jayde had no idea Nic would come back to Earth."

To be fair, she had a point. I recalled that fateful party where Nic had waltzed in and stopped Jayde from throwing me off a balcony. Judging by the fact that he'd panicked, Jayde had been just as surprised as I was to see Nic again.

No, Ephesus and Cea were probably right. If Jayde had a master plan to murder Nic, he certainly wasn't acting like it. But if it wasn't Jayde, then there was only one other person who could be responsible.

"Data," I murmured, then quickly clarified. "He's the one who programmed my chip."

More accurately, "Data" was his callsign; I had no idea what his real name was. I'd met him only briefly when he'd delivered the finished hardware. He was an active member of the Boston underground and a friend of Jayde's, and that was all I knew about him. He could have a dozen reasons for wanting Nic dead.

My blood ran cold when I remembered what other projects Data had been working on recently.

"I gotta go," I announced. "I need to call Stanyard. Dad could be in trouble."

"Whoa, don't hang up!" Ephesus lunged towards the camera, as if that could stop me from ending the call. "What's wrong with Dad?"

I breathed through my nose and tried to get my heart to slow down enough so I could explain. "Data's been helping with Dad's therapy. Stanyard told me that Data installed some kind of brain chip to help with Dad's speech, and he's been progressing really fast—*too* fast."

Our father, Dr. Smyrna, had also been recently raised from the dead, but his resurrection was a lot less miraculous than Nic's. Our father had been cryogenically frozen, and over the last month we'd been undergoing the arduous process of thawing him out. Physically, he had survived the procedure well. Mentally, however, there was nothing left of the man I'd once known as "Daddy." All his memories were gone—or at least they were inaccessible to him.

He'd also lost most of his speech and social skills. But when I'd called Stanyard yesterday, he'd informed me that Data and several others had been overseeing Dad's therapy. They'd installed something in Dad's brain to supplement his vocabulary, and he'd been making herculean progress. At the time, I'd praised it as an answer to prayer. Now, I wondered if I should have shared Stanyard's suspicion.

If Data was willing to kill Nic, there was no telling what he'd do to my dad.

"I need to call Stanyard," I repeated. "I need to make sure Dad's safe."

"Okay but," Ephesus inserted before I could make a move, "make sure Stanyard is alone when you talk to him, and tell him to keep it quiet until we can prove it."

I hushed and waited for him to explain.

"If you're right..." Ephesus shared a wary glance with Cea before continuing, "then we're dealing with an accomplished killer. That's not someone you want to anger before you've got a plan. And second, speaking as a programmer, he might not have had anything to do with Nic's death."

"What do you mean?" I questioned.

"We have no idea who all was involved in programming that chip. Dozens of people could have had access to that code. What's more, he might have bought the DNA from someone else. Maybe they gave him the wrong code intentionally."

"It could even be—dare I say it—a really unfortunate programming error," Cea suggested.

"But you don't think so," I pointed out, reading between the lines.

Cea looked up at Ephesus. He shrugged. "I just don't want to accuse a guy of murder before I look at his source code."

He was right. I had to be careful—especially since Data had his hands in Dad's brain. "Can you figure out who downloaded Nic's DNA? Trace the IP or whatever?" I asked.

"I'll see what I can find out," Ephesus said. "As soon as you get your chip removed, send the code to me—that will tell us a lot. Stanyard should also search the servers on base. See if he can find any emails, source code, anything."

"Okay."

"And Phil…" Ephesus sighed, and the emotion bled back into his eyes. "Keep me updated this time. Please."

Cea took that as her cue to leave. "I'll go find Sydney," she said gracefully. "Have him start searching the logs. We'll talk later, Phil." She stood up and gave Ephesus a peck on the forehead, then waved at me before stepping out of frame.

Ephesus waited until the door had shut behind her before speaking again. "Why didn't you call me sooner?"

There was no accusation in his voice, but my guilt more than made up for it. When this all started, I *couldn't* have called him; he was on a transit to Mars, which put him offline for nearly four days. And for several days after that, I'd been held hostage by Jayde with no way to call for help.

But that wasn't a watertight excuse, and I knew it. I'd been able to get online several times since then, and I hadn't even sent my brother a text. The truth was that I hadn't called my brother because the thought hadn't even crossed my mind. Not once had I considered involving Ephesus.

Probably because he hadn't been involved in my life for the last two years.

Ephesus seemed to be tracking the same thoughts. "Look, I know I've been MIA a lot lately, but I'm still your big brother. And no amount of warmongering will ever change that."

He cracked a smile, which I knew was an invitation to let him in. I struggled to return the gesture as I recalled the past few months and tried to figure out when I'd made the conscious decision to shut my brother out of my life. We'd been separated several times over the past two years; had I simply gotten used to him not being there?

"Philli," Ephesus prodded when I didn't give him the answer he wanted. "You can trust me. You know that, right?"

"Of course," I answered reflexively. "I've always trusted you, Ephesus."

"Then please, keep me involved this time. Call me immediately if there's any change, and talk to me before you go anywhere. Promise me you'll stay with the Tangs until we figure out what's going on."

I met his gaze. "I promise."

I tried to put as much intention into my words as I could, but it didn't land. He stared, lips pinched in a small frown like he didn't believe me.

I didn't blame him.

He finally relented with a sigh. "I'll keep my phone with me and my ringer on. I'll answer any time of day or night."

"I'll text you after I call Stanyard and let you know what he says," I offered. "And I'll call you after I meet with Jael tomorrow."

"Thank you." He looked into my eyes again. "I love you, Philadelphia."

"I love you, too," I said, and then ended the call.

I flopped back on the pillows. Tommy mewed and got up, coming over to rub against my side. I stroked him absentmindedly as I fought the unfounded urge to cry.

What was wrong with me? I'd spent the last month of my life leading a revolution, and I hadn't even involved my own brother. I hadn't involved anyone. I hadn't involved Cea, I hadn't involved Stanyard, and I certainly hadn't involved Nic.

Sure, for part of that time, I'd been physically unable to contact anyone. But it wasn't like that anymore. Ephesus was there for me; Stanyard was there for me; the Tangs and their entire church congregation were there for me. Even Jael was probably still on my side, and she was a powerful woman with massive resources. I had hundreds of people willing to help me.

So why did I feel so alone?

4: NIC

Getting raised from the dead is not all it's cracked up to be.

My mind didn't miss a beat. If anything, the hard reset of being knocked unconscious gave it *more* energy and focus, and now it refused to shut down. I probably could have solved world hunger had someone given me a pen and paper.

The rest of my body, however, was complaining very loudly about the fact that it had been deprived of oxygen for nearly half an hour. Every muscle ached in a way that shouldn't have been possible, and all my organs were laboring like they forgot how to do their jobs. Sneezing hurt, breathing hurt, *blinking* hurt, and I could feel every single beat of my heart like a sharp slap on the inside of my ribs.

But at least my heart *was* beating.

I looked at the monitor next to my bed and watched the jagged green line jerk across the screen. I was alive, and by all accounts, I shouldn't be. Every single doctor, lab tech, and cleaning lady in this hospital had come by my room to gawk at me and reinforce that fact. The nurses were getting downright annoyed. Every time they came to check on me, they seemed frustrated that there was nothing for them to do, as if they wished I would just keel over so the order could be restored to their universe.

In their defense, I almost agreed with them. I was bitterly aware that this turn of events obliterated every logical and illogical excuse I had not to jump on the Jesus train. It worked in perpetuity, too; fifty years from now, if I even thought about going my own way, all He'd have to do is remind me that I shouldn't be breathing, and I'd be left with no argument to stand on. He'd been smart and written Himself a blank check, and my life was the dividend.

I grunted and sank back on the stiff pillow. It was one thing to stand there and tell Phil that God had a call on her life. It was an entirely different matter to realize that God had pulled a Lazarus because He was so stupendously serious about the call He had on *mine*.

"I guess I can't change my mind now, can I?" I muttered to the empty room.

The answer was immediate. *You're going to want Me anyway.*

As if reinforcing the point, voices in Mandarin echoed in the hall, followed by the all-too-familiar clack of stilettos on linoleum. I groaned and rubbed my temples as a headache preemptively started thrumming behind my ears. "No rest for the wicked," I grumbled, even though I was aware that, as of a few hours ago, I no longer fit that criterion.

Without a warning knock, the door blew open, and my ex-girlfriend breezed into the room. "Nic! I was so worried!"

"Let me guess," I droned, "you came as soon as you heard—after you did your hair and makeup and got a manicure."

Asia had dressed for the occasion, as she always did. She looked like she'd walked right off the senate floor with her designer skirt set, patent heels, and signature bloodred lipstick. The outfit choice a power move, no doubt—and considering the fact that I was barely clothed in a hospital gown, it was working.

She reached up and patted the pearls she had pinned in her dark updo. "I always get dressed up for you, sweetheart."

I rolled my eyes. "I'm going to need you to at least put on a *pretense* of authenticity. You never called me 'sweetheart' even when we were dating."

She smirked and clacked over to the bedside. The stench of her perfume followed her like a wave of mustard gas. I gagged as my eyes watered; at least if I suffocated from the smell, the nurses would have something to do.

Asia perched on the edge of the bed and studied me. I sat up as best I could and plastered on a bored expression. Being bedridden in front of my ex was not a power balance I was comfortable with, but I was not going to give her the satisfaction of watching me squirm.

You know you can ask for My help, right? the Voice in my head inserted.

Asia spoke again before I could take Him up on His generous offer. "I came to tell you the good news, but I can see the staff has spoiled my fun." She flicked her acrylic fingernail against the handcuff that tethered my left wrist to the bed.

"Ah yes." I rattled the chain. "I was hoping you'd put in a good word to the warden for me."

She arched a waxed eyebrow.

"If they could assign me a number shorter than '120518,' that'd be great. You know how I hate long names."

A wicked grin spread across her face, revealing perfect teeth. "I'll slip a few hundred yuan to the clerk. But I haven't decided where I'm sending you yet—I'm still picking out which celebrities I want on the jury."

I stifled a groan. Unlike jail time, the fake trial was a cruel and unusual punishment I was *not* looking forward to. "Far be it from me to deny the public of their pomp and circumstance. Should I tell them about our tragic love story? That will really bring in the views."

"What love story?" she chirped with practiced innocence.

I sighed to acknowledge my defeat. While her list of accomplishments was not nearly as illustrious as mine, Asia was guilty of plenty of crimes—or, more accurately, she was guilty of *funding* plenty of crimes. Notably, she was the one who had given me the science station on Mars so I could develop Red Rain, my world-ending chemical superweapon. That alone would get her sent straight to the gallows—except I couldn't prove it. Asia had always been thorough about covering her tracks; even if I could get online, I wouldn't be able to find any digital evidence proving she'd been involved. It would be my word against hers.

And we both knew who her "celebrity jury" would believe.

"Face it, darling," she crooned, dragging a sharp fingernail along my tethered arm, "I'm over you."

I let all the air in my lungs out in a dramatic *whew*. "Took you long enough. You really should have seen a therapist about eight years ago."

She shrugged and stood up. "I still think you're cute, though, so if you get bored…" She winked and strode towards the door. "Besides, I'm hoping we can avoid a trial. It's always so much cleaner to settle out of court, and you know how I feel about an unnecessary mess."

My blood ran cold when I remembered what this was really about. Asia didn't care whether I lived or died, but she would hang me out to dry if it would blackmail Phil into blowing her cover.

"It won't work," I called after her.

She paused in the doorway and glanced back.

"As much as I'd love to see you go through this whole song and dance for nothing, I feel obliged to inform you that this evil scheme of yours will not work."

"Whatever do you mean?" she taunted.

"Phil," I said, and hoped none of the nurses were listening. "She won't come for me."

Asia cackled. "Have you no faith, doctor?"

Until earlier this afternoon, no, not really. "We've been practicing the whole 'obey your parents' thing. And even if she doesn't," I forced myself to admit that very real possibility, "she's smart enough to get her chip removed. You're not going to get what you want out of this."

I desperately hoped—prayed, even—that Phil would heed my warning and stay away. But even if she didn't, I knew she was in no danger of killing the General, accidentally or otherwise. Phil had made a lot of mistakes, but that was one I was confident she would not repeat.

Surely, Asia knew that. She was, regrettably for all involved, not an idiot. She had to realize that the game was up. If she wanted her father dead, she was going to have to do it herself.

Unless, of course, she wanted Philadelphia for something else.

Asia smirked, confirming my fears. "Nic, you surprise me. For someone with three PhDs, you're so narrow-minded."

I swallowed my next comeback. The game was not up; it had just started.

She relished my discomfort. "But then again, you always did underestimate me, didn't you?"

I lifted one finger. "Underestimated? No. Naively thought the best of you? Guilty as charged."

She smiled benevolently, as if she found my failure adorable. "I guess that's why I'm going to win."

I opened my mouth, but she didn't give me a chance to detangle that threat. She opened the door to the hall. "I'll come see you off when they discharge you. Get some sleep, sweetheart—you've had a long week."

And then she blew me a kiss and disappeared.

5: PHILADELPHIA

I lay on the bed, staring at the ceiling and struggling to pray, for so long that exhaustion almost claimed me. Thankfully, my tablet pinged with a notification, jerking me awake. I picked up the device and found a new message from Stanyard:

I CAN SEE YOU'VE READ MY MESSAGES. WHY HAVEN'T YOU CALLED ME?

I cringed and sat up. *Why do I always forget about that setting?*

Stanyard started typing again, but I hit the call button before he could finish. He answered on the first ring.

"Phil!" he gasped, the connection crackling as the call struggled to bridge the ocean between us. "Where are you? What's going on? Didn't you see my messages?"

"Yes, yes, I did." I raised my voice to be heard. "I'm sorry, I called Ephesus first."

He paused, long enough for his video to connect. The screen brightened, revealing my best friend in his natural habitat: in front of a computer. The dual monitors behind him were cluttered with a dizzying number of windows, and the backlit screens framed his unkempt dark hair in a blue glow as he pushed his headphones back. He spun his desk chair around and held his phone away from him so he could frown at the camera.

"I'm glad you talked to Ephesus," he conceded, "but you were supposed to call me twelve hours ago."

I flinched when I remembered I'd promised to call him when I got up this morning. I hadn't, since I'd been busy getting kidnapped, but I also hadn't checked in with him since then. I hadn't even sent him a text, and I'd had plenty of opportunities to. I'd just forged ahead, never once considering his feelings. I'd made a life-changing decision and put myself at risk, all without involving the people who cared about me the most—just like I always did.

"I know, I'm fine now, I promise. Stanyard, I'm so sorry," I insisted. But as soon as the words left my mouth, I realized we'd been through this whole song and dance before: I would apologize, he would forgive me, and then nothing would change. *I* wouldn't change.

He was slow to respond. I could tell by the tension in his jaw that he was very angry and struggling not to be. "What happened?" he said, skipping the preamble.

I took a deep breath. "There's not going to be an easy way to tell you this..."

"Please, Phil," he sighed. "Just tell me."

I swallowed a prayer. "Jayde... he..."

Stanyard jerked upright as every muscle in his body went rigid. "What did he do?" He was so furious that his words slurred.

"He... broke into the house..." The kilter of my voice pitched like a ship lost at sea as I struggled to put words to the trauma. "...drugged me and kidnapped me. He was going to make me record more videos."

Stanyard threw his device down and slammed his fist on the desk. I flinched as the camera shuddered. There was a flicker of silence, and then I heard him muttering. It took me a minute to realize he wasn't using English.

"Stanyard..." I called hesitantly.

"I knew this would happen," he snapped, but his voice wasn't angry anymore. It was broken, shattered like a dozen pieces of mirror, reflecting a jagged array of emotions.

"Stanyard," I repeated, "come back, please."

He picked up his phone. "I knew he would try something like this. I should have—"

"Should have what?" I cut him off. I knew exactly where this conversation was going. "There was nothing you could have done. You're not even on the same continent."

"I could be."

The statement was spoken softly, almost wondrously, as if the thought had just occurred to him. I looked down to see him frowning in concentration. "You're not really thinking of flying over here, are you?" I challenged.

"I am now."

"Stanyard, you can't," I objected. "Asia—"

"Could have killed me a month ago if she was so inclined." It was his turn to interrupt. "Frankly, it's not her I'm worried about. It's Jayde."

I almost agreed with him. Even though Asia was far more powerful than Jayde, she was at least a lot more civil.

"I know, but I promise, they're taking precautions. Jael..." I paused when I remembered Stanyard would have no idea who what was. *Add it to the list of information I unintentionally withheld from him.* "I've got a friend here with access to the algorithm. She's watching Jayde's file. She'll protect me."

"And what if Jayde's smart and starts using a temp file?" Stanyard countered, presenting a hideous possibility I hadn't even considered. "Or he's got other friends? Phil, this has gotten so big that I don't think anyone can protect you."

I stared at the blinking light of my camera as I realized he was right.

"But that's not going to stop me from trying."

I focused on his face again. I could see the red seeping into the corners of his eyes—the stress accumulated from hours of sleepless worry and frantic prayers.

"Philadelphia," he sighed, dragging out my full name to give us both time to gather our thoughts. "We can't keep doing this."

His statement dropped an unfamiliar weight on my chest. "What-what do you mean?"

"I mean I can't keep watching from the other side of the camera while you throw yourself into the path of speeding trains. I know you've got a reason for being in Beijing..." The statement came out condescending, and he caught himself. He worked his jaw and tried again. "I know you've got a call on your life, and I know what you're doing as Blue Fire is important. I still support you. Please don't take any of this to mean that I don't."

I nodded and tucked his statement away in my heart, knowing I would need it later.

"But I can't keep watching you die on live TV and then getting the synopsis via text twenty-four hours later. I'm not just a viewer on your videos, Phil. I'm your friend." There was a breath, and then he found the words he really wanted to say. "And I'll be a lot more than that if you let me."

"Yes," I breathed, the word coming out like a gasp as the air caught in my throat.

"Then you have to let me help you," he insisted, voice growing firm. "You have to let me protect you. It's my job."

His words sent warmth radiating down my arms, but I knew I couldn't let him jump on a plane to China just because he was worried about me. "I know, Stanyard, but there's nothing you can do—"

"You need to let me be the judge of that," he snapped. He groaned and ran a hand through his hair. "See, Phil, this is what I'm talking about. You can't keep making all the decisions and then just hand out information to me when you think it's important. If this is going to work between us, then we need to be partners."

I swallowed as an entirely new breed of fear wrapped its cold fingers around my neck. He'd said "if."

He shifted, as if aware of the burden he'd created. "Do you trust me, Phil?"

"Yes," I declared, and then realized, in a flash of cruel clarity, that wasn't the problem. "But can you trust me?"

His silence told me all I needed to know. I pinched my eyes shut as tears flooded the corners of my vision. *Oh God, where did I go wrong?*

"I know a lot has happened that neither of us could have controlled. I'm not blaming you *or* myself for that." Stanyard's voice reached out to me, gentle and forgiving. "And I know you did what you thought was right at the time."

He sounded confident of my character, but suddenly, I wasn't so sure.

"But I have no reason to believe that, as soon as we hang up, you won't run off and start another war—and I won't hear about it until it's too late."

His voice was so heavy with unfiltered pain that it took the wind out of my lungs. He truly *didn't* trust me—and I'd given him no reason to.

Ephesus was right. I should have called somebody—anybody—sooner.

I blinked, even though it did nothing to clear my vision. "What can I do to fix it?"

"Let me in." He leaned forward, like getting three inches closer could span the distance between us. "You have to start involving me. You say you trust me—so, start trusting me with things."

He made it sound simple, but as I replayed my actions over the past few days, I struggled to pinpoint what I would have done differently. Sure, I should have talked to him sooner, but what would that have changed? He couldn't have prevented what happened with Asia or Jayde. Maybe if I'd talked to Stanyard, I wouldn't have had a breakdown and shot somebody, but eventually I would have touched Nic and activated my chip. In a sick way, I wasn't sure *any* of what happened was avoidable—and if Stanyard had been here, he would have just gotten hurt in the crossfire.

And that was exactly why I couldn't let him come to Beijing now. Besides, I needed him on the ground in Boston.

"Well," I said, and tried to make my voice approachable, "there's something else I need to tell you."

He sensed my shift in tone and sat up straight. "What's wrong?"

I slowly walked him through the events of the day. He almost lost his cool again when he learned Nic was no longer with me, but I managed to keep the conversation on track.

"I don't think it was an accident," I finished. "I think someone is trying to kill Nic."

I paused and waited for him to turn back to the camera; his gaze was taking a lap around the room like it always did when he was struggling to process. When he finally looked at me again, I saw that his eyes were even more bloodshot than before. "You're probably right," he admitted, "which means you're in danger."

I didn't necessarily agree; just because someone wanted Nic dead didn't mean they would hurt me. But it definitely meant they weren't my friend. "That's why I need you to look at the servers on base. See if you can find any evidence that someone planned this."

"On it." He swiveled his chair around to face his desktop. The backlight from the monitors washed out his face as he propped up his phone and started typing.

"I'm getting my chip removed tomorrow and sending the code to Ephesus. I'll send it to you too."

He nodded, his eyes flickering as he focused on his screen. "If Jayde hasn't changed his password, I might still be able to hack into the door lock software and see if it was him who downloaded Nic's DNA."

The more I thought about it, the more I agreed with Ephesus; Jayde probably had nothing to do with Nic's death. But it was worth a look. "There's one other thing I need you to do," I added.

"Yeah?" he said, the word nearly drowned out by his aggressive typing.

"I need you to keep an eye on my dad."

He stopped and faced the camera.

I let out my breath and tried not to release all my anxiety with it. "Data's the one who coded my chip. And you said he's been working on my dad."

I could tell by the way Stanyard's expression darkened that my fears were not unfounded.

"Ephesus said it might not be him," I added, mostly for posterity. "Other people could have worked on that code."

"Possibly," he grunted without consent. "But if it was Data, I'll find out."

It was a threat—and in some strange way, that made me feel safer.

"How was Dad today?" I asked.

Stanyard's eyes cleared as he blinked away the anger. "Better. I think he's coming to terms with his new life. He's been more patient when we try to teach him new information. You can tell it means nothing to him—it's all just random facts—but he's more willing to listen."

I managed a smile and thought about asking to see him—then realized, with a stab of guilt, that I didn't want to. I couldn't manage a third broken relationship tonight.

"What are you going to do now?" Stanyard's question cut through my daze.

"What do you mean?" I returned, even though I immediately knew where this road would lead.

"Are you staying in China?"

"I have to find out what they're going to do with Nic," I said, which wasn't an answer and definitely not the one Stanyard was looking for.

"And then what?"

I didn't have a response, because untangling that question involved speculating about the morbid details of Nic's fate. And while I ultimately had no idea what Asia would do next, I knew in my heart that Nic would not be getting out of prison anytime soon—if ever.

And I wasn't ready to live in a world without him.

No, God, please—there has to be another way! I thought, for the first time since the accident finding the words to pray. *This can't be how it ends.*

All of that emotion must have made it onto my face, because Stanyard dropped the subject. "We'll figure it out, Phil, I promise."

There was no point in acknowledging that. "I need to go," I said, knowing that if I didn't concoct an excuse to end the conversation, Stanyard would never hang up. "I promised to text Ephesus after I talked to you."

He accepted that and leaned away from the camera. "I love you, Philadelphia. And I'll always be here for you."

"I know," I mumbled, and was surprised when my voice shattered. I quickly hung up before he could see the first tear fall.

6: PHILADELPHIA

John and Dowe woke me before my alarm did.

"Phil. Philli!" one or both of them hissed through my door. "Are you awake?"

Not by choice, I thought to myself as I groaned and pushed the blanket aside. Tommy contorted his body in a terrific stretch, then jumped off the bed and pranced to the door. He mewed and scratched at the frame.

"Tommy's awake!" John crowed, losing all concept of an inside voice. "Go get your mom out of bed, kitty."

"I'm up, I'm up," I mumbled. I groped for my house shoes in the near darkness; judging by the lack of light bleeding through the shutters, it was barely sunrise. What were they doing here so early? "What do you need?" I groused, fully aware I was being saltier than necessary.

"Uh, come outside, and then we can talk," one of them returned, which wasn't ominous at all.

I sighed and opened the door—and almost screamed when I came face to face with their identical grins. They were both standing unacceptably close to the door, crammed shoulder to shoulder in the narrow hall, like they were a jack-in-the-box that could spring out at any moment.

"Wow, hi," I managed, leaning back. "What are you doing?"

"We know it's early," John said in a voice still too loud for the time of day. They were both fully dressed and looked like they'd been up for hours, not that I'd ever seen either of them act tired.

"That's why we brought a peace offering." Dowe held out a mug of coffee with both hands. With slow, dramatic movements, he bowed and set it on the floor at my feet. Then both he and John folded their hands and backed away slowly, like they'd just made a sacrifice at a shrine. They looked so ridiculous, with their hips scraping the wood paneling as they stumbled over each other, that I couldn't help but laugh.

"Ceasefire accepted," I said, and bent to pick up the mug.

Dowe grinned and elbowed his partner. "Told you! It works on Nic, too."

I smiled sadly at the steaming liquid as the memories invaded my groggy brain. Picking up Nic's coffee habits had been an accident, but, just like our unexcepted relationship, it was something I didn't regret adopting.

I took a slow sip. "What are we doing up so early?"

"We called our mechanic, did some sweet-talking," Dowe said.

"*I* did some sweet-talking," John interrupted. "She hung up on you!"

"It was a bad connection!" Dowe argued, then looked back at me. "Anyway, we got an appointment to get your chip removed—but it's all the way across town, so Lanzhou wants to head out before rush hour hits."

"Which, on a weekday, is about 5am." Lanzhou stumbled out of his bedroom at the top of the stairs. He shrugged on a jacket and offered me a sleepy smile. "Better take that coffee to go—we've got some walking to do."

After spending five minutes convincing John to leave Tommy at home, we started the long trek across the sprawling city. Even though the crowds hadn't fully woken up yet, it still took us over an hour of transferring between buses and subways to reach our destination. Lanzhou was armed, and I kept my hood up and my head down, but I wasn't really worried. Most of the Chinese populace didn't know I was here—yet.

The commercial district we found ourselves in was on the bleeding edge of downtown. The high rises were so tall that they blocked out the rising sun, making the street seem dark and chilly like a cave. A glinting array of neon and automated vending machines struggled to modernize the concrete buildings and backlit signs that had clearly been there since the last century. The narrow storefronts competed for attention with a circus of flapping banners, while lanterns and flags strung across the road added to the noise. The whole place was loud, cluttered, and colorful, but after being in Beijing for a week, I was surprised at how comforting the chaos was beginning to feel.

John and Dowe led us to a phone repair shop at the end of a long alley. The only part of the store's banner that was in English were the words "KIMCHI MOBILE," but the intent was made clear by the fact that every inch of the windows was plastered over with posters advertising the latest devices for suspiciously low prices. I felt a bit guilty thinking it, but it definitely looked like the kind of place where someone would try to scam you into buying a knockoff watch.

The door buzzed as we entered. I took one look at the place and almost walked back out. To say the shop was a disaster would have been putting it kindly; it looked like a shipping container of electronics had gotten upended in the store. The smudged glass display cases were crammed with refurbished phones, while stacks of laptops balanced precariously on the shelves. Every flat surface was strewn with hard drives and broken keyboards, as if a serial killer had gutted a dozen computers and left the corpses to rot.

I was suddenly feeling much less confident about letting this woman dig into my hand to remove a very delicate bomb. *Oh Jesus, I hope this is the right choice.*

The young clerk behind the counter put his own phone down long enough to wave at us. "Ahh! You here for the latest phone? We've got the 87S, very new—70% off, just for you!" He turned his grin on me, as if correctly assuming that I was the one with the most disposable income.

Dowe planted his hands on the counter. "No, no, we're here to pick up a *custom order*... if you know what I mean."

John folded his arms and jerked his head in a way that was probably supposed to look cool but came off as anything but. "It's under the name John Dowe."

The clerk glanced at his monitor and clicked a button, then crooned in understanding. "You have an appointment?"

"I have a lifetime subscription," Dowe intoned.

"Very good... this way." The clerk lifted the gate and waved us behind the counter. John and Dowe went first. I had to suck in my breath to keep from knocking over a pyramid of computer towers as I squeezed through the narrow hallway to the back of the store.

We followed the clerk into the storeroom. He kicked aside a box, revealing a trap door. The secret entrance had clearly been retrofitted; the shiny metal panel was at least fifty years newer than the building, with a massive latch and a blinking keypad. It looked like something out of a space station, which somehow made me even more uneasy.

The clerk pressed his thumb to the keypad, and it chirped welcomingly. The lock released with a hiss, and he threw the panel back, revealing dimly lit concrete stairs. He gestured at John and Dowe to lead the way, which they did eagerly.

I hesitated at the top of the stairs. "I'm right behind you," Lanzhou whispered in my ear, but even I could tell he wasn't thrilled by the prospect.

I muttered a prayer and started down the steps. The clerk stared at us until we had cleared the entrance, then slammed the door. I heard the lock slide shut with a loud click. Shivering, I ran the rest of the way to the bottom.

Beneath the store was a massive workshop. It was a huge space—at least four times the size of the sales floor above—but there was barely room to walk around all the mechanical paraphernalia. The owner of the workshop was clearly a jack of all trades and a master of none; a glance around revealed at least a dozen abandoned projects. There was a vintage car with its engine gutted on one side of the room and a wingless helicopter on the other, and the skeleton of a robot dangled from the ceiling by thick wires. The stuffy air reeked of grease and freshly fabricated plastic, and an abundance of fluorescents lit the room as bright as noonday, making the place buzz like a hornets' nest.

Dowe stepped forward and rapped his knuckles on a worktable. "Seoul? You in here, beautiful?"

A screeching voice echoed from somewhere across the room. "Don't you *dare* try and flatter me!"

Something crashed into the wall behind Dowe's head and clattered to the floor. I looked down to see a rusty wrench skid across the stained concrete. *Did she just throw something at him?*

Dowe sidestepped so he was partially hidden behind a stack of boxes. "I take it you missed me?"

She was not appeased. "Some nerve you have coming in here after you didn't pay me!"

"I paid you!" he protested.

"Not enough!" she shrieked back. I saw movement from behind the broken helicopter and turned to see a young woman emerge. She was in her twenties, but she was at least half a foot shorter than me and looked like she couldn't have weighed more than a sack of rice. Her boyish hair was dyed an electric shade of blue, which contrasted sharply with the orange tracksuit she wore. She had goggles strapped to her forehead and two utility belts hanging off her thin waist. She was distinctly Asian, but I could tell by her accent that she wasn't from around here.

She aggressively wiped her fingers with a rag, then threw the cloth on the floor. "I told you, I'm not doing any more work for you until you repay me with interest—oh, hi John."

She broke off mid-sentence to smile at him. He wiggled his fingers. "Hi, Seoul."

Dowe gaped at his partner. "Is there something I should know?"

"What's there to know? He tips." Seoul skipped over to John and stood on her tiptoes to plant a kiss on his cheek. He reddened and beamed like she'd just scratched his favorite spot behind the ears.

Dowe huffed. "I don't even know you."

Seoul ignored him and turned to me. "Now who's this?"

I started to offer my hand, then remembered why we were here. I settled for a polite bow of my head. "Blue Fire."

She whistled. "You boys are working for Blue Fire now? How'd you lie your way into that job?"

John shrugged. "She needed a distraction."

"As a matter of fact," Dowe inserted, "we were her first partners—"

Seoul cut him off with a flick of her hand. "Still not talking to you." She focused her attention on me again. "I heard a rumor that you were in the city but didn't realize you were working with these saints. What brings you to my shop?"

I held out my right palm. "I need an implant removed. Careful—it's reactive to touch."

She grunted and pulled her goggles down over her eyes. She snapped her finger against the side of the eyepiece, and the device whirred to life, a maze of blue code reflecting on the lenses. She leaned over and scanned my hand. "And what exactly was the purpose of this contraption?"

"It's an assassination weapon." I winced; it felt uncouth to talk about it so forthrightly, but if she was going to remove the chip, then she needed to know what she was dealing with.

"Who were you trying to assassinate? Godzilla?" she mocked. "This thing is juiced. I could probably power Jimin with this battery."

"Jimin?" John questioned.

She gestured at the robot hanging from the ceiling.

"Well, you're welcome to keep the battery if you can get it out," I said. "All I need is the code off the programming chip."

She pushed her goggles back on her forehead. "Add 10,000 yuan, and you've got yourself a deal."

I glanced at Lanzhou. Thanks to my inheritance as a Nolan, ten grand—in any currency—wasn't a sum even worth mentioning, but until we could figure out a way to launder my money without Asia knowing, the Tangs would have to front the bill.

Lanzhou nodded. "Get it done."

"We're going to need mood music for this." Seoul clapped her hands, and K-pop music started blaring from one of the computer terminals at a volume too loud for comfort. The anti-government lyrics were an angsty mix of English and Korean and were somehow strangely appropriate for the illegal activity going on in the shop.

Seoul gestured at a rusted metal chair next to a workstation. "You, sit. The rest of you, make yourselves at home—but don't you dare touch my car." The threat was directed with a glare at Dowe.

He opened his mouth to object, but Lanzhou shepherded them over to the other side of the room. I sat down in the chair and tucked my backpack underneath, then obediently laid my arm on the cold metal table.

Seoul turned on a spot lamp and shone it over my palm. After glancing to make sure the others were out of earshot, she leaned over and whispered, "Look, I'm sure you get this a lot, but it's an honor to meet you."

I had, in fact, been getting that a lot lately. "Thanks for your help," I deferred.

She went in for a handshake, then reconsidered. She settled for a sloppy salute instead. "Name's Seoul, in case you missed it."

"Like the city?" I guessed, finally putting two and two together with her accent. Although, "former city" would have been a more accurate term for the crater that represented the defeated South Korean capital.

"It was my parents' subtle way of protesting the North Korean takeover. Never mind that happened twenty years before I was born." She grinned, and the sharp lighting from the lamp made the gesture look mildly terrifying.

I shifted back in the chair to restore some personal space. "We all do our part."

She mercifully took the hint and turned to open a tackle box that was sitting on the table. "Now that we've gotten acquainted, I'd better be at the top of your contact list. Anything you need, you just call me. Don't bother with those other guys down the street."

"Thanks, I won't," I repeated, not that I had any idea who the "other guys" were.

"If it has a wire, I'm your girl. Phones, laptops, cars, implants..." She rooted through the tools in the box, tossing what she didn't need aside.

I watched her carelessly hurl implements on the floor and remembered what John and Dowe had said about getting work done. I glanced across the workshop, where they had gathered a pile of tools and screws and invented some impromptu board game. Lanzhou sat between them, looking utterly confused and more than a little bit unnerved.

"So..." I ventured, making sure my voice was low enough not to carry across the room, "how do you know John and Dowe?"

"Doesn't everybody know a John Dowe?" she quipped, then laughed at the exhausted joke. "They came asking for my help after the government botched their neurosurgery."

I stiffened at the mention of the all-too-familiar punishment. "They've been through neurosurgery?"

"Trust me, the government has tried *everything* to get those two to shut up." Seoul glanced at me. "They didn't tell you?"

I shook my head. John and Dowe hadn't been forthcoming with their personal history. Although, in their defense, I'd never actually *asked* about their past.

"They probably forgot." Seoul pressed a button on a mini power tool, and it whirred violently. "To be honest, I'm surprised they lived to tell about it."

As was I. I knew two other people who had been through neurosurgery: Nic's parents, Mr. and Mrs. Von Nieuwenhuyse. According to Nic, they'd both been brilliant scientists prior to the procedure; Mr. Von was almost single-handedly responsible for putting humans on Mars. But all of that had been erased when Asia had them convicted for religious noncompliance and put under the needle. She'd done it to try to convince Nic to complete Red Rain. She succeeded, but Nic found out who authorized the procedure and broke up with her.

The Vons had survived the surgery physically, but their minds were shattered. I'd lived with them for a month when I was last in Boston, and the only way they could function was by developing precise patterns. If there was even the slightest deviation from the status quo—like me coming home five minutes late—they had a nervous breakdown.

John and Dowe were hardly neurotypical, but compared to the Vons, they were doing brilliantly. They at least remembered people and events from the past six months; the Vons couldn't even remember their own children.

I looked down at Seoul. "But how… how can they remember stuff?"

She bowed and spread her hands dramatically. "One of my finer projects."

"I don't—I don't understand," I said.

She grabbed a rag off the table and splashed some rubbing alcohol on it. "I installed experimental brain implants that helped restore some of their memories. I say 'some' because they got aftermarket prototypes—cheapskates."

I struggled to process what I was hearing. A hundred undead hopes resurrected and created a hurricane in my chest. If John and Dowe were functioning on Chinese knockoff versions of this device, then what was the original implant capable of? Was it possible that the Vons could be brought back from the dead?

"How does this implant work?" I asked.

"The logic is fairly simple, honestly." She picked up a tool and started sanitizing it with the rubbing alcohol—although seeing as the cloth was stained with grease, I wasn't sure the device was getting any cleaner. "Neurosurgery doesn't erase memories. It just rewrites the neural pathways so people aren't triggered by things the government deems problematic."

I knew that was true; I'd read as much in a medical journal while studying the Vons' condition. Instead of brainwashing the victim and starting with a clean slate, neurosurgery was supposed to "cut out" the noncompliant parts of a person's psyche. The theory was that you could delete the Christian or the revolutionary but keep the doctor or teacher. The problem was that it almost never worked.

"Think of it like snipping the wire to a light bulb." Seoul demonstrated with a clack of the tiny shears she had in her hand. "The light bulb's still there—there's just no power going to it."

I was beginning to catch on. "So, if you can reconnect the power…"

She grinned. "Exactly. Unfortunately, repairing the neural pathways themselves is an art we haven't quite mastered yet. But a synaptic device doesn't need any fancy neurons to access those memories."

I frowned and waited for her to explain.

"It's a combination of two very basic technologies: synaptic reading and augmented reality." She shifted through the junk on the table until she found two pieces of circuit board, then turned to face me. "The synaptic device reads the stored memories," she held out one piece of circuitry in her right hand, "and the reality augmenter projects it to the mind." She held out the other piece of circuitry in her left hand, then smashed the two together.

"You can bypass the damaged neurons entirely," I murmured.

Seoul muttered a proud *mmhmm* and tossed the circuit boards back on the table. Taking the same alcohol-soaked cloth, she grabbed my arm and started sanitizing my hand.

I numbly let her work. My heart was pulsing as I remembered who else had a damaged brain.

My father.

I looked down into Seoul's eyes, begging her to tell me this was all true. "You can bring someone back. You can restore who they once were."

She contorted her face in a disheartening gesture. "Sort of. It's not flawless, and it takes a lot of programming before the device really starts working. You have to 'teach' it what memories you want it to pull for certain words."

"What do you mean?" I asked, struggling to swallow my heart as my hopes plunged back down again.

"Think of it like a search engine. If you say 'daughter,' it's going to scan the memory banks and pull up *all* images associated with that word. It's really overwhelming at first, and there's no order to the results. You have to train the algorithm, and even then, sometimes it gets it completely wrong."

I looked over at John and Dowe, who were bickering over what number their makeshift die had landed on. "Is that why they're…?"

"They're what?" Seoul prodded.

I struggled to come up with a polite way to say it, but there was no polite way to describe the mental state of John and Dowe. "Well, most people, when you tell them you need a distraction, would reach for a flare gun, not a can of whipped cream."

Seoul laughed. "Oh no, Dowe's always been creative like that. And John… well, it's not really his fault. He's the second."

"Second of what?" I demanded.

The question apparently wasn't important enough to answer, because she kept blathering on. "No, their problem is they bought fake implants off a scammer. Their chips can only hold about a dozen terabytes of information. As soon as you learn something new, *poof…*" She fluttered her fingers like a fleeing bird. "There goes something else important. Like how much you owe your mechanic."

She paused to stare at them, but I could tell by the tweak in the corner of her lips that she wasn't really mad. "Thankfully, the technology has come a long way in the last few years, or so I've heard."

That was all I needed to hear. "I need three of these devices."

She dropped whatever she was holding. "What?"

"I need three of these implants," I repeated, "as soon as possible."

"Okay, first of all." She took a step back and punctuated with both of her hands. "There is no 'as soon as possible' on the black market. You get what you can when you can get it. And second of all—"

"I thought you said you were 'my girl' when it came to anything with a wire." I arched my eyebrow in a gesture Nic would have been proud of.

She halted with her mouth open. "Okay, erase that list and start over. New first of all: That's rude."

I shrugged.

She growled and tensed her muscles in a pose that would have been threatening had she been more than five feet tall. "Fine. Then let me put it this way: These devices are extremely illegal and use extremely rare components. That means they're extremely expensive."

"Money is no object," I replied, and it really wasn't. "Besides, if that's the case, then it seems a job like this would warrant a pretty hefty finder's fee, wouldn't it?"

She blinked as every muscle in her body relaxed, and I knew we had a deal.

"And if adding an extra zero doesn't provide the necessary incentive..." I traced my finger through the grime on the worktable. "You can tell them Blue Fire sent you."

"That... might actually work," she admitted. She let out a puff of breath, causing a stray chunk of her blue hair to flop into her eyes. "All right, fine, I'll do it. I make no promises that I can get three of them—but I'll start making calls."

"That's all I ask." My voice was calm, but my mind was anything but as my soul whirled out of control. Would this work? Could we bring the Vons and my father back from the dead? Would I finally be able to put my family back together? Seoul claimed the devices weren't perfect, but any memories would be better than none. I would spend the entire Nolan fortune if it would bring even a piece of my father back.

The Holy Spirit pressed down on my chest, and I took a deep breath. As much as I wanted to drop everything and save my father, I knew I had to trust Seoul to do her job. I wouldn't know who to call about one of these devices even if I could safely get online. There was nothing I could do but wait—and pray.

I closed my eyes and started doing just that, and hard.

"Well," Seoul chirped, ending the subject like one closes a book, "let's get you disarmed before you blow up a rhino with this thing."

I looked up just in time to see her snap a magnetic clamp over my wrist, pinning it to the table. She tugged on a pair of gloves, then yanked her goggles over her eyes. Grabbing the tiny shears, she reached for my finger, then hesitated.

"Oh, I should probably warn you." She glanced at me, her expression unreadable behind the code flickering across her lenses. "This is going to hurt a lot."

7: PHILADELPHIA

In a cruel irony, removing the implant took twice as long and hurt three times as much as installing it.

The procedure was excruciating. I blacked out once and almost vomited multiple times. John and Dowe did their best to try to entertain me, but even they weren't distracting enough to keep me from crying in pain. The whole ordeal took over four hours and involved more than a little blood.

To make matters worse, Seoul wasn't even able to remove the whole device. She claimed extracting the wiring would be too dangerous, and after seeing the state of her workshop, I didn't want to push my luck and lose my whole hand. Instead, she removed the programming chip and the battery, then cut into each of my fingers and snipped the wires in multiple places.

I was disheartened by the fact that I would still be carrying the fragments of a bomb in my body, but Seoul assured me that it would be impossible for anyone to reconstruct the device. If someone wanted to turn me into a weapon again, they would have to install brand new wiring.

Seoul finally released the clamp that held me down. I lifted my hand slowly, afraid to look. With a prayer, I rallied the courage to open my eyes—and was surprised to find that my palm looked unscathed. The newly regenerated skin was flawless, each incision fully healed. I flexed my fingers and felt all my nerves respond; they weren't even numb.

"Thank you," I said with more than a little admiration.

Seoul winked. "I told you I was your girl." She walked over to one of the computer terminals and yanked a flash drive out of the port. "Here's the code."

I shakily stood up and reached to take the drive. I slid it in an inner pocket of my backpack and zipped it shut. *Hopefully, this will give us some answers.*

"And here's the chip."

I looked up. Seoul rooted around on the table until she found a small plastic case of nails. Dumping the nails out on the table, she dropped the chip in the container, snapped it shut, and held it out to me.

I almost didn't take it. Why would I want to keep the bullet that had killed Nic? It took everything in me not to throw the chip on the floor and stomp on it. But I knew I should keep it until we figured out what was going on; Stanyard or Ephesus might need more code from it.

I forced a smile and accepted the container, dropping it in my backpack. "Thanks," I mumbled.

"Anything for Blue Fire," she said, and grinned.

Lanzhou paid her, and then we eagerly climbed the stairs and left the store. I stumbled out onto the sidewalk, breathing deeply. The air in downtown Beijing wasn't much cleaner than the air in the shop, but I was grateful to see the sun again.

"We need to hurry back." Lanzhou gestured and led the way towards the bus stop. "Jael is waiting to see you."

I flinched when I remembered I still had one more apology to make. "What did you tell her?"

"She knows about Nic and your chip." Lanzhou glanced back at me. "I figured I'd leave the rest to you."

I rubbed my arm. I had no idea how merciful Jael was, but I knew *I* wouldn't be lenient if a crazy teenager shot me in the chest at pointblank range. Thankfully, it was going to take us an hour to get back to the factory—and that gave me an hour to find my own forgiveness.

Holy Spirit, please help me make this right.

It was well into the afternoon by the time we returned to the factory. The Tangs owned a business on the river downstream from their home. Over a decade ago, Mr. Von had granted Mr. Tang an exclusive contract to produce a specialized part for space stations, and the Tangs had profited handsomely. In exchange, Mr. Tang agreed to let an underground church meet in his building. That venture had also been extremely successful, judging by the crowd I'd seen at the service two days ago.

First shift was grinding to a close as we arrived. The dock gates were open as a trickle of office workers fled the scene, eager to beat rush hour. Bowen met us in the lobby and led us past the noisy locker rooms and up an elevator to the third floor.

Jael was waiting in the same conference room we'd met in the day before. She presided in the same chair at the head of the table, one leg crossed over her knee in the same regal pose, as if she'd been waiting all day for my arrival. If it weren't for the fact that she'd changed her skirt set and rotated her heavy ensemble of jewelry, I would have thought she hadn't moved at all.

She rose when I entered. "Philadelphia, you've returned." Her Hausa accent made her words so thick that I couldn't detangle the emotion behind them.

I halted just inside the door, suddenly wishing I could be anywhere else. It didn't help that I'd forgotten how imposing Jael was, with her tall heels and crown-like turban.

She flicked her hand. "Come here."

I somehow found the will to obey, walking to the end of the conference table and stopping a few feet in front of her. Lanzhou and Bowen followed at a safe distance.

Jael waited. When I didn't initiate, she arched an eyebrow. "Is there something you want to tell me?"

"Jael, I..." I sighed. All my prepared speeches evaporated, replaced by a meek and simple: "I'm sorry."

"You are forgiven," she announced. "Now, why did you do it?"

I jerked back. "What?" I hadn't expected to reconcile that quickly—or to have to produce an explanation for my actions.

"You shot me, child." She stared at me with an expression that was neither angry nor amused. "For the safety of all involved, I think it's important that we both understand why you did it, so it doesn't happen again."

I struggled to put my insanity into words—and that's when the Holy Spirit answered my hours of prayer. "I did it because… I felt used. You took my image and built a war around it, and you never asked my permission. We hadn't even met."

She accepted the accusation with a slight shrug. "And?"

"And what?" I returned. That seemed like reason enough to shoot someone—or at least it had, in the moment.

"If you were only upset about being made into the thunderbird, then you would have shot Jayde a long time ago." A hint of a smile made it onto her face. "No, Philadelphia, you've made peace with Blue Fire. She isn't the problem. So, I ask you again: What is?"

I searched my soul and found the answer I had been too afraid to share with anyone but Nic. "I broke down because… I thought I'd made a mistake. All this time, I thought God was the one who had created Blue Fire and made my videos trend. I thought it was a miracle."

I scrolled back through the inconceivable events that had transpired over the last six months and tried to find the same sense of wonder I'd had before. I shook my head. "And then I find out it was just you controlling the search engine the entire time. I felt like a fool and wondered if I'd gone through all that pain for nothing."

Bowen moved in my peripheral. "Of course, it wasn't for nothing. You—"

Jael lifted a finger to stop him, her eyes still on me. "And how do you know God wasn't also speaking to me?"

I looked up and met her gaze.

"Philadelphia, no one's denying that this has been hard on you. Lanzhou and I both agree: Our meeting should have been handled differently. But this revolution isn't about you. It's about freedom. And if you want to have a part in saving the world, then you're going to have to accept that you're but one piece of the puzzle. Things are going to happen that are outside of your control. People are going to make decisions without you— including me."

Her bright heels clicked on the floor as she closed the gap between us. She laid her hand gently on my shoulder. "I'm asking you to join a war, not lead it. Can you follow? Can you learn to take orders from me?"

I swallowed as apprehension made my throat go dry. "What do you mean?"

"Blue Fire works for me, not the other way around," she announced without ceremony. "I'm the one leading this operation, which means I give the orders. If I tell you to record a video, you smile for the camera. If I give you a script, you read it. If I tell you to stop and wait for directions, then you don't move until I tell you to."

I searched her face and tried to grasp what she was asking me to do. She was asking me to surrender, to put my identity in her hands and let her write the script. The way she saw it, this was her revolution, and I was just another soldier in her army. Blue Fire was hers to control—and I had to trust that she was using my image for good and not evil.

Was that what God wanted? Was that why He had brought us together?

"Because if you can't do that, you can go home."

"What?" I gasped more than spoke as I jerked out of my thoughts.

Her expression was devoid of emotion. "You're seventeen— eighteen if you ask Andromeda. I won't make you sacrifice your life for this if you don't want to. If you can't handle taking orders, I can get you off the grid and send you back to Boston."

"No!" I shouted, more loudly than I intended. I couldn't leave Nic, and I knew giving up was not what God wanted. Nic literally had a vision about me being in Beijing, as a Nolan, fighting Asia. I may have messed up God's original plan by trying to kill the General and getting Nic arrested, but I still had a purpose. I was still Andromeda Nolan for a reason. If Jael hadn't given up on me, then I wouldn't give up on her.

"No," I repeated, more resolutely this time. "I want to help. Tell me what I need to do."

A genuine smile finally broke Jael's expression. "That's what I needed to hear, soldier. I want you to record a video today, just a short one. Your followers need to know you're alive and well, and that you want them to await further instructions."

She turned and strode back to the table. I stumbled after her, suddenly dizzy. *That's it, then?* After days of running and questioning God, it was disorienting to suddenly find myself back where I started, recording videos as if the last week never happened. It was like someone had reset the game and dumped me at the beginning of the level.

"I've written a few remarks for you to cover—you can embellish them how you see fit." Jael picked a tablet up off the table. "But first, there's something you need to see."

She swiped on the screen, and the projector in the back of the room brightened to life. The elaborate device projected a 3D rendering of the contents of Jael's tablet against the blank wall. I gripped the back of the nearest chair as a larger-than-life picture of Nic consumed the screen.

It was a bland, washed-out shot in front of a white wall: an intake photo. Nic glared stoically at the camera as his uncombed hair cast defiant shadows on his face. The orange collar of his prison jumpsuit stuck up on one side, as if he couldn't be bothered to fold it down.

I bent over the chair as all the guilt and regret threatened to push themselves back up my throat. I knew Nic would get sent to prison, but it still hurt to see it emblazoned on the screen in ugly, undeniable orange.

Nic, I'm so sorry. I did this.

"His trial is scheduled for next week," Jael said softly.

"Next week?" Bowen sputtered. "You can't even get a parking permit that fast. Mong must really have a grudge."

She does, I thought, shuddering. *Against me.*

"What are they charging him with?" Bowen asked.

Jael shook her head, her gigantic earrings drifting listlessly. "Classified."

"Can you do anything?" Lanzhou ventured. The question was directed at Jael, but there was no hope in his voice.

"I haven't been able to find out where she's holding him." There was a pause, and I could tell by the pinch in her expression that Jael was just as despondent as the rest of us. "But I promise, my people are on it." She shifted her gaze to me, watching for my reaction.

I pushed myself upright, then hesitated when I noticed some highlighted text in the corner of the projection. I pointed. "What does that say?"

Jael turned her head to follow my finger. "They've set bail."

"Bail?" I gasped as my world doubled over again. "You mean we could—"

"That's not bail, that's extortion," Lanzhou interrupted. "That's an astronomical amount."

I stepped closer to the screen and squinted at the numbers. There was an excessive number of zeros at the end of the sum, enough that it felt like a made-up figure.

Bowen slammed his fist on the table. "That's insane. No one could pay that."

"I could."

It was only when everyone stopped to stare at me that I realized I'd spoken aloud. I straightened as hope ram-rodded my heart. "I can afford that—Andromeda can. I can bail him out of jail. We need to—"

"Absolutely not." Jael's command was cold, callous. "You will not be bailing him out."

"But we have to! I can't let Asia—"

"*Asia* is the one who's watching your bank accounts. If you show up to post bail, she'll be right there to catch you."

Jael had a point, but surely there was a way around that. "Then help me launder the money. Someone else can post it—I just need you to help me transfer it. You control the algorithm. Surely, you can hide a transfer."

Her hesitation told me that she probably could, but she shook her head. "It won't solve anything. Even if he gets out on bail, he'll still have to show up for trial—and I can guarantee you that Asia will be tracking him very closely. If you bail him out, she'll follow him straight to you."

I braced myself on the table as helplessness washed over me. "But I can fix this," I murmured, mostly to myself.

"It would be a waste of money," she said, tone only one degree warmer than heartless. "This is not the first time I've fought Asia, so I know her tricks. She's baiting you, Philadelphia, and you cannot afford to fall for it."

She was right, of course, but that just made the situation even more agonizing. Asia was doing all of this because of me. The trial, the outrageous bail—this was personal. She was manipulating the chess board to ensure that the only way to save Nic would be for me to turn myself in.

And it was only going to get worse.

"No matter what happens to me, no matter what you hear, I need you to promise that you won't come for me. Do you understand?"

"If you want to help him," Lanzhou touched my arm, "the best thing you can do is record a video."

I looked up. Bowen nodded at me from across the table. "Do your part. Let Jael manage the rest. She'll figure out where he's being held—just buy us time."

I turned back to face her. She lifted one eyebrow. "Can you handle this, Philadelphia?"

I sucked in a breath through my nose. If fighting for Nic meant becoming Blue Fire again, then that's exactly who I would be. "Yes," I declared, and hoped my voice came off more confident than it sounded to my own ears. "Put me on air."

"Excellent." Jael clapped her hands like a judge banging a gavel, ending the discussion. "Everyone, back to work. Internet usage is going to peak in a little over an hour, so if we're going to hit that window, we need to move. Philadelphia, go get dressed."

"Get dressed?" I repeated. I glanced down at my ripped jeans and nondescript t-shirt; what was wrong with what I was wearing?

She flicked a bejeweled finger at my bleached blonde hair. "You can't go on camera looking like a Nolan."

She had a point. If I was going to record videos again, then I had to bring Philadelphia Smyrna back from the dead. But that would be easier said than done when I didn't have any makeup or supplies; I didn't even have a change of clothes, except what I'd borrowed from the Tang daughters. Nic and I had fled into Beijing with nothing but some water bottles and a blanket.

"I may be able to help with that."

I turned to see Bowen approach. He held out a black duffle. "Narissa sends her regards."

I took the bag hesitantly. "But how did you..."

"Nic mentioned her. I figured if you were going to be staying while, you'd need a wardrobe change, so I put in a special order." Bowen grinned.

I caught myself returning the smile. Narissa was my stylist; she'd designed the gown I'd worn at the state dinner. She'd also helped us get a head start on Asia by letting us out a back way and distracting the guards. I trusted her, and she certainly did know how to make me look good.

"Follow me." Bowen gestured and led the way out of the conference room.

I shouldered the duffle and followed him down a floor to a private bathroom. After thanking him, I locked the door and set the bag on the counter.

For the first time since yesterday, I paused to really look at myself in the mirror. Andromeda Nolan stared back. A bleach job, blue contacts, and three ear piercings attempted to transform me from an unassimilated criminal into a societal elite—and so far, it had worked.

I squinted at my face. My right cheek was faintly red. I gingerly touched it—and remembered.

Jayde had slapped me on the face yesterday. I'd prayed that it wouldn't bruise, and it hadn't. It wasn't even tender anymore.

I murmured a prayer of thanks, but somehow, I wasn't surprised. The whole situation seemed almost mundane. After all, I'd seen a man raised from the *dead*; a bruise was inconsequential.

I stared at my fingers as that thought disrupted something in my soul. Then I shook off the feelings and turned my focus back to the task at hand. I unzipped the duffle and discovered Narissa had crammed an entire dressing room into the bag. There were several outfits, two pairs of shoes, and a pouch of makeup. I chuckled; since I couldn't get to her studio, Narissa would send the studio to me.

I unfolded the top outfit. It was a pair of army green cargo pants and a matching jacket. It was paired with a black mock-neck tank top and fingerless utility gloves. I fingered the sturdy linen fabric of the pants and fought down a wave of trepidation. The outfit looked like something a military officer would wear— which was, I suppose, exactly the look we were going for.

I quickly changed before I could second guess myself. I turned to the mirror and realized that the tank top proudly showed off the thunderbird tattoo I had on my right shoulder. The thunderbird symbol—a silhouette of a black hawk with a bolt of blue lightning clutched in its talons—was the icon of the revolution and the brand that permanently marked me as "Blue Fire." Narissa, as always, had thought of everything.

Something had to be done about my hair, however; most of the internet still thought Philadelphia had a long dark brown mane. I rooted around in the bag until my hand closed around a soft package: a wig.

Inside was a handwritten note:

I CAN'T FIX THAT ABYSMAL BLEACH JOB, BUT AT LEAST I CAN COVER IT. –N

P.S. SORRY ABOUT Q. LET HIM TAKE CARE OF HIMSELF. YOU'RE DOING THE RIGHT THING.

I blinked back a stray tear and desperately hoped she was right about the last part.

I pulled the wig out of its plastic packaging. The long, fake hairs were a chocolate brown color and done up in a twisted bun that was somehow both elegant and demure at the same time. A single curled strand was left to hang loose against the left side of my face.

After pinning my short hair back, I slid the wig on. The look was convincing—no one on the street would be able to tell that it wasn't my natural hair—and I was surprised at how much the refined style aged me. With a little bit of eyeliner, I could pass for twenty-five. I looked bold, confident, mature.

Everything I wanted the internet to see.

I reached for the makeup pouch, then noticed there was something else tucked in the corner of the bag: a jewelry box. I opened it and found a hairpin made with a real feather. The barbs were black and flashed iridescent blue in the light, like a raven.

The symbolism was not lost on me. This was a thunderbird feather.

I pinned the accessory against the base of my bun. Closing my eyes, I took a deep breath and prepared to face my old self in the mirror.

But when I looked up, it wasn't Philadelphia Smyrna who was staring back at me.

It was Blue Fire.

8: NIC

They kept me in the hospital for "observation" for another twenty-four hours, probably so that they could add an extra zero to the bill. By then, I was so inhumanely bored that they were at risk of needing to readmit me to the psychiatric ward.

Turns out, the high-security jail cell Asia had prepared for me was almost the same thing.

The space was so narrow that I could touch the opposite walls at the same time. The door was eight inches thick, and beyond that was a gate that dropped down like the airlock on a space station, blocking out the light from the hall. There were no windows, because criminal geniuses can't be trusted with such things—not that there would have been much of a view. Judging by the long elevator ride down, the cell was several floors underground. They probably designed it that way so that if I should somehow figure out how to drill through the solid steel walls, I'd hit only bedrock.

But just in case the earth's crust was not strong enough to contain me, they added an ankle bracelet. Asia came to watch them fit it, grinning gleefully like we were trying on wedding outfits.

Her smile vanished when I told her this was the only "ring" I'd ever wear for her.

The cell was painted solid white, which in itself was a form of torture. As if that wasn't mind-numbing enough, there was also a TV tuned to the United's usual fare of fake news and censored sitcoms.

I kept the device off for the first three days. I preferred to go insane the old-fashioned way: by talking to myself in the mirror. Besides, Asia provided more than enough entertainment. She visited me at least twice a day, giving me updates on my court case like she was planning our honeymoon.

"I'm legally obliged to tell you that they've set bail," she informed me after I settled in. "Not that you can afford it."

"This is why you always paid for dinner," I replied with a shrug. But I knew who could afford to post bail: Andromeda Nolan.

It was a cheap shot, but I couldn't blame Asia for trying the bloodless option first. I prayed that Philadelphia wouldn't take the bait, and for the first time in a decade, my prayers were answered. The week blurred into the weekend, and there was no word from Andromeda.

By then, even Asia's conversation was starting to sound intellectually stimulating, so I knew I had to resort to drastic measures before my mind cracked.

I turned on the TV.

I scrolled through the stations, changing the channel whenever the programming became too stupid to bear. That worked for about forty-eight hours, but the tide of insanity was gaining momentum. I scrolled faster, my finger punching the button like a woodpecker, desperate to see the image shift, the colors flash, for there to be any change in my environment whatsoever.

And that's when I saw her.

Philadelphia.

I almost scrolled past her, but her voice pulled me back. She was broadcasting on some obscure local channel, a gimmicky shopping network the censors probably forgot about. Jael must have hijacked the signal.

Phil sat in a chair in the center of the frame. She was in a nondescript office, with a map adorning the wall behind her, like she was a stateswoman issuing a speech. Through some fashion wizardry, they'd brought her brown hair back. A layer of makeup concealed the circles under her eyes, and smokey eyeshadow added eight years.

She looked halfway to thirty, and I hated it.

"The rumors are true," she narrated, clearly reading prepared remarks. "My position was compromised."

"That's an understatement," I grunted at the TV.

"But I can assure you that I'm safe—and I have no intention of giving up this fight. Operation Blue Fire is still on, and we need your help more than ever."

She leaned forward, and I saw the same glimmer in her eyes that she'd had when she'd spoken in church a week ago. It was that moment of possession when Philadelphia left and Blue Fire took over.

"They're calling this a 'petty demonstration'—but we know that's not true. Operation Blue Fire is not another riot. This is not some march around the capital where we hold signs and scream at politicians who will never hear us. We don't need the government to wake up—we need *the people* to wake up."

She's getting closer, the Voice in my head commented, abruptly reminding me of His presence.

Closer to what?

But she needs you to get there, He said, which didn't even remotely answer the question.

Phil's recording spoke over both of us. "This is about saving a generation. If we don't do this, then our children will just repeat the cycle—and there will be no end to the United."

She looked down, picking at the remnants of polish on her fingernails. "But we can end it. We can stop the cycle. We just have to be brave enough to be uncomfortable."

The sparkle faded from her eyes as she faced the camera again, her voice becoming rote. "Operation Blue Fire continues as scheduled. Await further instructions, and please forward this video. Thank you."

She fell silent, and for a second, I thought the playback had paused. But then she shifted, and I could tell by the change in her tone that she was going off-script.

"Q." Her voice halted, like she hated saying the nickname as much as I hated hearing it. "I don't know if you're seeing this, but..."

I involuntarily stood up and stepped closer to the screen.

She brushed a strand of hair behind her ear and looked straight into the camera. "But if you do... I'm sorry."

And then the video looped, cutting back to the beginning of her speech and starting over.

I threw the remote across the room. When it didn't break, I picked it up and hurled it into the wall—again and again until chips of plastic started flying off. The image on the TV glitched and changed channels before finally going dark.

"It's not supposed to be this way!" I yelled, my voice tinging irritatingly off the metal walls. "She needs me—You even said so Yourself!"

He had, in fact, said that—a mere five minutes ago.

"Yeah, well, you know what I'm doing right now? *Not* helping. In fact, I'm no expert, but based on circumstantial evidence, this is just making things worse."

It was. As much as I hated to admit it, I was playing right into Asia's hand. Even if Phil was smart enough not to fall for Asia's trap, she was no doubt watching the proceedings. She'd witness my trial unfold on TV and blame herself for the whole debacle. And if there was one thing I knew about Philadelphia, it was that she would let guilt grind her into the dirt until there was nothing left of her soul.

And that's when Asia would win—thanks to my help.

"You can't let that happen! Are You just going to let Asia use me like this, after You went to all the trouble of bringing me back to life? Because that seems like a waste of a good resurrection."

I looked up at the ceiling and spun in a circle, half-expecting Him to pop out of a corner. "I have to get out there and help her!

That's the whole reason You dragged me back to this stupid planet!"

I didn't use the word "stupid"—and that's when I realized that yelling at the King of Creation was probably not the most effective way to get an answer.

I sighed and pinched the bridge of my nose. "Look... I need You."

The words tasted disgusting—although that was probably on account of the sacrilegious tone I'd used to say them. I spat in the sink and tried again.

"I can't do this by myself. I'm sorry it's taken being locked behind eighteen inches of steel and a mile of bedrock for me to admit that, but here we are. If You want me to help her, then You're going to have to get me out of here."

As if in response, the gate outside the door groaned open.

I whipped around. "That... wasn't the answer I was expecting, but I'll take it."

There was beeping as someone typed on the door's keypad. The door squeaked open, and I was more than a little disappointed to see Asia standing in the hall.

And I thought we were having a real moment there.

She tossed a stack of clothes at me. "Get dressed, and don't make me wait."

I caught the clothes and shook them out to find a halfway decent suit and button-up. "What's this for? Is it Tuesday?"

"It's actually Monday," she intoned, missing the joke, "and you need to look nice for the judge."

My good mood faltered when I realized the worst of my punishment was about to begin. I started unbuttoning the shirt. "I hear they'll give you a lighter sentence if you wear fake glasses."

"I'll see what I can conjure up. In the meantime, wash your face, and *please*," she coated the word with enough drama to win an Oscar, "shave that hideous mustache."

I grabbed the door handle. "You'll have to convict me first." And then I slammed the door in her face.

After I took as long as humanly possible to tidy up—which is harder than it sounds when you're a guy—Asia cuffed me and loaded me into the back of a police van. We drove across town and parked in an underground garage. As soon as we got off the elevator, I recognized where we were: the Supreme Court Building in Beijing. Clearly, Asia had pulled out the red carpet for this event.

She herded me to the lobby. Even though I couldn't see past the line of guards, I could hear the thrum of a commotion outside. Half a dozen police stood with their backs braced to the front door, as if they were afraid someone was going to break in.

Suddenly, I knew what was going on. And for the first time since my arrest, I felt the tiniest bit afraid.

Asia's deadly fingernails scraped my forehead as she tried to straighten my hair for the third time. "Remember, keep your chin up, eyes forward. Smile for the camera."

"Why should I?" I snapped.

She sneered. "Because your daughter is watching."

Then, at the flick of her finger, the guards dragged the double doors open, releasing the onslaught of cameras and press.

The flash from a hundred bulbs was so blinding that it lit the foyer like a lightning strike. I instinctively shielded my face as my vision washed white, then black.

"You'll ruin the shot!" Asia protested, yanking my arms back down.

Someone shoved me forward onto the step. A gaggle of reporters clogged the stoop, shouting their inane questions over each other.

"Dr. Von Nieuwenhuyse!"

"Over here!"

"Please, sir, a statement!"

I stared out at the throbbing mob as the whisper of fear grew louder. I looked inward and struggled to hear the Voice in my head over the noise.

So, you know that miracle we were just discussing?

He finally responded. *Yeah?*

I'm going to need it now.

"Dr. Nic!"

I made the mistake of turning in his direction. The intrepid reporter took that as an invitation to elbow several people out of the way and come stand in front of me. "Sir, are you aware of the charges laid against you?" he demanded.

I actually wasn't; that was a minor detail Asia had left out of her incessant gabbing. "I'm going to need you to rephrase the question," I grunted, unwilling to admit my ignorance on live TV. "My teleprompter is broken."

The chatter of the crowd finally stilled, as if everyone was waiting to hear the reporter's reply. He held his microphone close to his lips as he shared my darkest secret with the world.

"The environmental weapon, sir. They're saying you invented Red Rain."

9: PHILADELPHIA

I didn't sleep for a week.

There was no word on Nic. His file was never updated; all it said was that he had been arrested and the initial hearing set for Monday. Jael searched every device connected to her company's network, looking for information on his location or the charges laid against him, but found only rumors. It wasn't like the information was classified; Jael might have been able to hack into it. It was like the information was never recorded. Whatever Asia was planning, she had been very careful not to leave a digital trail.

I knew why. Asia hated an unnecessary mess. If she had her way, she'd bargain with me quietly, and Nic's arrest would never make it onto the news. His court date was the ticking time bomb between us: I had until Monday to turn myself in before she made him suffer.

But I couldn't fall for it. Stanyard and Ephesus both repeated the sentiment when they heard the news; even Cea called and, in her own grief-stricken way, gave me permission to essentially abandon her brother. Every time I asked Jael if there was any new information, she closed the conversation with a platitude like, *"You're making the right decision,"* as if she correctly assumed I was drowning in doubts.

I let silence be my response. I couldn't agree; to make a conscious decision to walk away from Nic, to verbally admit I was leaving him behind, felt like signing his death warrant. So, for five long days, I did nothing.

I couldn't even sleep. No matter how much I prayed, no matter how much I paced the room and tried to make myself tired, darkness never came until it was too late. I would snatch a few broken hours before sunrise, and then the restless cycle would begin all over again as soon as daylight peered through the shutters.

I didn't know what was wrong with me. Why wasn't prayer working? Talking to the Lord had always brought me peace in the past, but not now. I tried listening to worship music, I tried reading the Bible, I even tried crying and pounding the floor. Nothing worked. It was like all my thoughts and emotions were locked in a glass coffin. No matter how much I screamed and banged on the walls to get out, nothing changed.

I didn't tell anyone. I was afraid that if I told the Tangs I wasn't sleeping, their doctor would try to give me more sleeping pills, and I didn't trust myself on medication. So, I lied my way through breakfast every morning and used concealer and extra coffee to cover up what was really going on.

It was a cruel mercy when Monday finally rolled around. I arrived in the conference room at the factory to find everyone gathered in front of the projector.

Jael turned to me as I entered. "Bad news."

"What? What's wrong?" I threw my backpack on the table and shoved past the others to stand next to her.

"Asia brought friends." Jael stepped aside and pointed at the screen.

Live footage of the Supreme Court Building was rolling. A mob of reporters clogged the lawn, vying for position in front of the steps, while the alarming words "Breaking News" scrolled across the ticker in English and Mandarin. The anchormen in the studio gossiped about who or what could have the government in such an uproar.

"Every station is playing this," Jael explained. "She stopped all the regular programming."

I bent over the back of a chair as a wave of seasickness crashed into me. Our time was up. As soon as Nic walked out those doors, his life would be over.

Just then, the courthouse doors opened. The crowd erupted like a pot boiling over. At first, there was such a jostle of bodies and microphones and drone-guided cameras that I couldn't even see him. But then a guard shoved him onto the top step, and the footage focused on his face.

He stood there, blinking as the flash of a dozen bulbs drowned him in harsh light. He squinted at the crowd, like he couldn't figure out where he was or why he was here. He looked lost, confused.

My heart went to my throat. I'd seen Nic display a lot of emotions, but confusion was never one of them. He always put on a façade of being in control, even when he wasn't. But in that moment, as he involuntarily stared at the camera, I could tell that he was just as afraid as I was.

Suddenly, I understood how Stanyard felt. Watching from the other side of the screen while someone I cared about was raked across the coals was the worst kind of agony—especially when I knew it was my fault.

There was motion in the background. Asia walked out of the courthouse, looking immaculate as always. She took up station in the shadows next to the door and scanned the crowd, feasting on the chaos.

I clenched my fists.

The reporters continued to shout unintelligibly over one another. I couldn't make out a single word as their questions muddled into an aggressive mess. Finally, the reporter from the station we were watching managed to elbow his way through the crowd to the foot of the steps.

"Dr. Nic! Are you aware of the charges laid against you?"

Nic turned towards him. The crowd took that as their cue to quiet as everyone waited for his answer.

"I'm going to need you to rephrase the question. My teleprompter is broken," he muttered, the sarcasm a weak attempt at self-defense.

The reporter gestured for his camera to come closer. Nic's face filled the screen in high definition as the reporter gave him his sentence.

"The environmental weapon, sir. They're saying you invented Red Rain."

Someone gasped, but it wasn't me. For one breathless minute, nobody moved, not even Nic. It was like the video had frozen. Then, perhaps involuntarily, he glanced back at Asia.

She smiled.

"No! Stop!" I screamed as everything restarted in a rush. I lunged forward, believing for a wild moment that I could reach her. I tripped and landed in the middle of the projection. The colors flashed around me as the mob ignited again, their frantic shouts shrieking in my ear like a hurricane.

"You can't do this," I sobbed, even though I knew she could, and she had. The only reason Asia had kept Red Rain a secret for so long was because Nic was useful to her.

But he wasn't useful anymore.

Someone pulled me to my feet and hauled me back. I let them guide me to a chair as Jael barked orders and people began to move in all directions.

Nic struggled to face the camera. "I don't know what you're talking about," he returned, answer stiff and practiced.

The reporter was prepared. "Then it's not true that you've been using your science station on Mars as a cover for your operations?" he challenged.

Nic's stunned silence told him all he needed to know.

I gagged. I slapped my hands over my mouth as the world spun out of focus. *Oh God, no. Not the base.*

Even though the truth was plainly written on Nic's pale face, the reporter was persistent. "What do you have to say to these accusations, doctor?" he demanded. His voice was so calm, like he had no appreciation for the destruction he was wrecking with his words.

Nic stiffened. The clarity returned to his expression as he set his jaw. He looked above the reporter's head, straight into the camera lens—as if he knew I was watching from the other side.

"Warn Klez," he ordered. "Tell him Code 2319. Tell him to—"

Someone shouted an objection. The police reacted; I saw guards lunging towards Nic while press people scrambled, and then suddenly the image went dark.

I scrambled up. There was a flicker of static, and then the broadcast cut to the anchormen in the studio as they hastily apologized about "technical difficulties."

Murmurs ignited around the room. "Who's Klez?" Bowen asked me.

"My brother." Klez was my brother's callsign. I sucked in my breath when I realized what Nic was trying to tell me. "We have to warn them!"

The commotion in the room increased. "Warn who? Philadelphia, what's going on?" Lanzhou demanded.

I ignored them all. I grabbed my backpack off the table and fumbled with the zipper. *Oh God, please don't let it be too late!*

Jael stepped closer and watched me.

I yanked my tablet out of my bag. I almost dropped it as I scrambled to dial Ephesus. It rang once, twice, three times.

"Please pick up!" I shouted, shaking the device.

He did. He was sitting at a desk, typing casually on the computer. "Hey sis," he greeted, only one eye on the camera. "Everything okay?"

"No!" I shrieked. "You need to get out of there. They're coming for the base!"

Jael turned and started issuing orders.

Ephesus set his mug down and gave me his full attention. "Whoa, who's coming? What happened?"

I took a deep breath and slowed my words. "Nic's trial— they've implicated the station. Asia told them about Wing 74."

He blinked while he ran that information through his internal processors—then he shoved his chair back. The camera jerked as he took off running. "Cea! Cea! Laodicea!"

"What?" she screeched from off-screen. I heard the *whoosh* of a door, and her voice came through more clearly. "What's gotten into you?"

"Asia told the court about Red Rain and Wing 74," I explained, loud enough for them both to hear me. "The government's coming—they're going to investigate. Nic told me to warn you."

She stepped into the frame. "When did this happen?"

"Just a few minutes ago."

"Then we've got a few hours." Ephesus kept his voice steady. "The nearest settlement is at least three hours away."

"No, that means we have thirty minutes," Cea snapped. "We need to be out of here and far enough away that they'll have difficulty tracking the vehicles."

Ephesus's stalwart expression wavered. "But where—"

"Nic has a friend who owns a mining operation on the other side of the quadrant. It's extremely remote—no one will find us there. It will take a few days' drive, and we'll have to navigate the old-fashioned way. No GPS, or they'll be able to track us." She laid a hand on his arm. "Nic planned for this."

"Nic also said to tell you 'Code 2319,'" I inserted.

Cea gasped.

Ephesus looked down at her for an explanation. She went pale as she relayed, "That's the emergency code to wipe all the servers—even Wing 74. You'll essentially factory reset the entire base."

I failed to breathe as I registered what that meant. It wouldn't be just Nic's illegal projects that would be lost. My brother's work, the Bibles Nic had in his media archive, all the scientific experiments that had been conducted on the base since its construction—over a decade of work, erased like a chalk drawing.

Ephesus inhaled and found his courage. "There will be some physical evidence in Wing 74 that I won't have time to destroy, but it will keep a couple of people's files clean." He grabbed Cea's shoulder. "Make an emergency broadcast to the entire base. They have thirty minutes to be in the docking bay, or I can't guarantee their safety. Tell them to bring only what will fit in a backpack— it's going to be tight. I'll handle the servers."

Cea nodded and disappeared.

The camera bounced as Ephesus took off running again. "As soon as we hang up, you need to delete me as a contact and wipe your call history," he ordered, voice jagged as he pounded down the hall. "I don't know how thorough this system reset is, but you don't want any record that you ever talked to anyone on this base."

"I will," I promised, even though my voice was shaking.

"Call Stanyard and tell him to do the same with the servers in Boston—and then they need to make themselves scarce." Ephesus looked down at the camera, as if making sure I was paying attention. "If Asia is willing to sacrifice this station, then the base in Boston is probably next."

I gasped as the insidious possibility seized my soul. I glanced across the table at Jael; she was already swiping furiously on her tablet.

I heard a door open and a sharp crack as Ephesus threw his device on a desk. I could just barely see him moving on the edge of the frame as he bent over a computer terminal.

"Ephesus, I'm so sorry," I called. "This is all my fault. What are you going to—"

He wasn't listening. The computer screeched at him, and he growled. "You're going to have to authorize this. My security clearance isn't high enough."

"What?"

"The emergency wipe requires Level 2 security access or higher—you're going to have to do it." He picked up the device and flipped the camera so I could see the computer screen. A bright red warning confirmed his statement.

"I have security access?" I wasn't aware I had any clearance on the base at all.

"Nic gave you Level 2," Ephesus said, his voice sounding distant from off-camera.

I stared at the text on the screen as this admission warped my reality. That meant the only person with a higher security clearance than me was Nic. He'd entrusted the entire station to me.

And now I was going to use that power to destroy it.

"We don't have much time." Ephesus punched the button to run the program.

"Voice authorization required. Please state your name," the computer intoned.

"Andromeda Nolan," I answered reflexively.

The computer chirped and flashed a cruel, ironic green. It prompted Ephesus to specify a time limit, and he typed in thirty minutes. The screen locked, displaying only a ticking time bomb as it counted backwards. I whimpered when I realized what I'd just done.

Ephesus paused, as if he, too, abruptly realized there was no going back. Then he flipped the camera back around so I could see him. "I'm going to be offline for a few days until we get there," he explained.

All the grief dropped to my stomach as I realized this situation was bitterly familiar. *No, not this again.*

"Stay off the grid and don't go anywhere until I can call you again," he continued to dictate. "Keep a low profile and don't let anyone know where you are."

"But Ephesus, I—"

He was already on the move. "Keep your head down," he repeated, and hung up.

10: NIC

The base was gone.

Asia forced them to run the story on the news for several days, playing the clip over and over until even the liberal anchormen were tired of talking about it. The raid wasn't even exciting, thanks to Ephesus's quick action. By the time federal agents got to the base, it was deserted, all the servers wiped clean. As a final insult, Ephesus had shut off the generator, taking the environmental controls offline. It took the government two whole days to restore the pressure so they could get in the building, and then all they found was damaged equipment, frozen experiments, and dead plants.

Base #9.6.11 was ruined.

I told myself I shouldn't cry over spilled milk. After all, Asia was the one who had given me control of the station; it was only a matter of time before she took it away. But as the clip of federal agents breaking down the door of *my* house played over and over, I realized logic couldn't cauterize this wound.

That base represented my entire life's work. In between my various attempts to take over the world, I'd accomplished some glorious science; my office was plastered with awards and commendations for experiments I'd overseen. "Governor" had been my identity for a decade, and now I had nothing to show for it.

What aggravated me most was the senselessness of it all. Destroying the station was a waste. Since Red Rain had been deleted, nothing sinister had gone on up there; the most illegal thing on the premises was Ephesus himself.

But Asia didn't need him or the data from my servers; she had more than enough evidence on her own cell phone to convict me. No, she had done this simply to be cruel. It was a last-ditch effort to get either Philadelphia or me to break.

After staring at the white walls of my cell for another five days, I was forced to admit that she almost succeeded on the latter.

Even though my guilt was undeniable, she still made me suffer through the spectacle of a trial. For three days I sat under the scrutiny of cameras as she paraded my sins before the court. Sensor logs proving I had been in Thames's office, security footage from Rott, data she'd salvaged from old servers—every piece of evidence she could present without incriminating herself was thrown at me like rocks at a stoning. By the time she rested her case, the entire world knew just how evil "Dr. Nic" was.

I considered trying to implicate her. I knew it wouldn't work, but I would have done it just to give her more paperwork to slog through. But, in a rare moment of foresight, the government was smart enough not to let me speak for myself. I'd proven I couldn't be trusted with a microphone at the press conference. Instead, they kept me behind a plexiglass booth for the entire trial, staging me like a museum exhibit while Asia and her hired witnesses dragged my reputation through the mud.

When Asia was finally done burning me at the stake, they tossed me back in my cell to await my sentence. The typical punishment for my crimes was death, but I knew Asia had other plans.

She finally came to visit me. I heard the door open but refused to turn around.

"Your sentence has been issued," she said when I did not initiate. "Seventeen consecutive life sentences, if I counted correctly."

"How many judges did you have to bribe to get that light of a punishment? I was expecting at least twenty-five. I'll have to modify my will."

She grunted. "Thanks to your little 'phone a friend' stunt, there wasn't enough evidence, so I had to drop some of the charges."

"Don't lie to me!" I yelled as my anger overruled my defenses. "You and I both know you didn't need evidence to convict me."

"No, but it would have saved me a lot of paperwork," she snarled.

I raked a hand through my hair. "Why? Why did you do it?" I didn't want a real answer, but I had to say something. Someone had to acknowledge how revolting this whole situation was. "You didn't have to involve them."

"I didn't have to involve your parents, either." She delivered the wound effortlessly, like a papercut.

I slammed my fist into the wall. "Phil wasn't even on the station!" I knew I was giving Asia exactly what she wanted, flailing my emotions about like some stupid circus animal, but "caring" hadn't made it onto my to-do list for the day.

"I'm just eliminating possibilities." She sighed, sounding exhausted.

I glanced over my shoulder and realized she looked terrible—for her, anyway. Other women would have killed to be her even in this state, but by her standards, she looked positively undone. Her unwashed hair had been plastered into a prude bun, and her makeup was beginning to peel. But most telling was the fact that she'd traded her murderous stilettos for demure pumps. The heel was so short that even Phil probably could have walked in them.

Mortality wasn't a weakness Asia displayed often, so the fact that she was willing to look human in front of me could only mean one thing: She'd failed.

Phil hadn't come for me. That meant she was still safe, and Asia had gone through this whole song and dance for nothing.

She'd invested time, money, and extortion into this ridiculous court case—and now she would have to clean up her own mess.

The thought gave me so much joy that my soul returned to my body. I straightened and clapped my hands. "Well, it's been terrible seeing you, but I've got work to do."

"What?" she screeched, jerking out of her own pity party.

"I don't know what your plans for the weekend are, but I've got seventeen life sentences to fulfill. Which, if I've done my math right..." I counted on my fingers, "...is about five hundred and ten years. So, if it's all the same to you, I'd like to get started."

*

It took us over twenty-four hours by high-speed train to reach my new prison, which gave me some concern. Once I escaped, it would take me a month to hitchhike back to Phil.

But the walk was only one of the many logistical problems I had to solve. The other issue was the altitude.

The prison sat atop a snow-covered mountain. From the train platform at the base of the range, I could just barely see the blackened steel structure clinging to the side of the peak like a leech. It looked like the building had washed up there during Noah's flood, and the enterprising communists had just taken advantage of it.

The terrain was so impassable that they hadn't even attempted to build a road. Instead, we followed a tunnel into the center of the rock and boarded an elevator. The elevator was a solid steel box with airtight doors like a submarine, and as soon as we started to ascend, I understood why. Had the elevator not been pressurized, all the vessels in my brain probably would have burst as we shot to twenty thousand feet above sea level.

As it was, the first thing I did when I stumbled off the elevator was vomit. Judging by the state of the vestibule, it was something of a tradition for new arrivals.

They herded me into a receiving area, where they forced me to change into an orange jumpsuit (not sure what was wrong with the one I had on) and took a thumbprint scan and a DNA sample. I then had the unique pleasure of throwing my ankle bracelet in the incinerator.

"I like you guys better already," I commented to the guard, to which he actually smiled.

The camaraderie expired when the secretary approached me with a gun. Without ceremony, she grabbed my right arm, pressed the barrel to my wrist, and fired. I yelped as something cold and sharp bit my skin like a staple.

"Nice to meet you too," I muttered, as a substitute for the choice words that came to mind.

She let go of me and frowned at the tip of the gun. "Oh, I forgot to sanitize that. I hope the last guy I used it on wasn't sick."

"Don't worry, I've had all my shots." I rubbed my wrist and felt a tiny metal capsule shift beneath my skin. "Let me guess: If I leave the premises, this device will explode."

She snorted and walked back to her desk. "No, it will just give them a beacon to find your body in the snow."

I sighed. "Glad to know they don't litter around here."

She used two pointy artificial nails to key a command into her computer terminal. "0118 999 881 999 119 725," she announced.

"What are those, your digits?" I snarked, even though I had a sinking feeling in my stomach.

"No, they're yours."

I facepalmed aggressively. "I would expect nothing less."

"Oh sorry, I read that wrong. It's 0118 999 881 999 119 725..." she squinted, "3."

"Have you *no* mercy?" I shouted at the ceiling.

The secretary lurched. "Excuse me?"

I wagged my head. "Not you. I'm talking to the Voice in my head."

Personally, I think it's hysterical, He replied.

"Well, come on then, let's get to work." One of the guards shoved me out the door. He prodded me down the hall and through another airlock into the main area of the prison. I stumbled onto the walkway, stopped, and stared.

"Keep moving," the guard yelled.

"Hang on." I put up both hands. "I have to appreciate this view."

The prison was an engineering marvel. It was built like a silo, with rings of rooms circling a hollow center. The structure was so tall that I could see neither the top nor the bottom; there must have been at least a hundred floors. But what was truly impressive was that they'd retrofitted the entire structure into a factory. Each floor housed a different enterprise as materials were ferried up and down the center of the silo by a network of elevators. It was like someone had taken an assembly line and made it vertical. The cavernous space throbbed like the inside of an organ as workers flowed in and out and the elevator chains danced.

"I could get used to a view like this," I murmured, then checked myself. "Yup, I'm used to it. God, I want a factory. Preferably one that isn't also a prison."

I can arrange that.

Wait, are You serious?

Are you?

"Glad to know you like the accommodations," the guard interrupted. "Now come on."

His tone of voice had changed into a threat, so I decided to obey. We got on an elevator and ascended another umpteen floors. My stomach protested the additional two hundred feet of altitude, but I managed to keep the contents inside.

We stepped off the elevator just in time to watch a guy get murdered.

I heard the infernal screeching even before the doors opened and thought it was the elevator in need of grease. The doors parted to reveal a stocky female officer exacting vengeance on a prisoner. She had him backed up against the railing as she lectured him with both her words and her firsts.

"How many times do I have to tell you, keep the plasma at a precise 563.28 kelvin!" The officer's Russian accent made her screams sound utterly barbaric.

The hapless prisoner was dumb enough to open his mouth. "I-it's at 563.27, miss…"

"I can read the dial," she snapped, "and that one hundredth of a kelvin could ruin the entire machine! Do you know how much this equipment is worth?"

"N-no," he chattered.

She grunted. "More than you."

And then in one karate-like move, she picked him up and hurled him over the railing.

We all stood still and waited for his screams to stop. I'm not sure they ever did; I think he just fell out of hearing range.

Wow, who threw off her groove?

"Now, why did I do that?" the officer groaned. She turned to the nearest guard. "When I got up this morning, I told myself I wouldn't kill anyone today—and now look. It's not even noon."

"I'll put it on your tasks for tomorrow, ma'am," the guard replied demurely.

"Thank you, you're such a gentleman." The officer looked up and spotted us. "What do you want?"

My escort shoved me forward. "This is the one Mong sent over. You asked to see him when he arrived."

Oh great, my reputation precedes me.

The officer sized me up. "What did you do? Dump her?"

I saw no point in denying it. "Actually, yes."

She cackled. "I would have too. I'm the warden here. You can call me warden, or if you're trying to get on my good side, Warden Ivanova."

"Thanks for the tip, Warden Ivanova," I returned with a salute.

She smirked. "You look like a smart boy with good survival instincts. How would you like a job?" Without waiting for an answer, she turned and gestured to the spot at the machine that had just been vacated. "Can you figure out how to run an interdimensional plasma fabricator, or do I need to show you the tutorial?"

"I prefer to learn by doing." The truth was that I could probably *build* an interdimensional plasma fabricator, given enough time and super glue, but I decided not to burden her with that information.

"I like your attitude," she praised. "What's your designation?"

I cringed. "I haven't memorized it yet."

"Then make one up." When I hesitated, she shrugged. "Don't waste too many brain cells on it. I won't remember it."

I groaned and took the obvious bait. "Q."

She hummed. "Short, a little mysterious—I like it." She turned to go, and the guards fell in line behind her. "Welcome to Russia, Q. Don't cause trouble, and we won't have to talk to each other ever again. Sound good?"

She didn't expect an answer; the door on the elevator closed almost before she finished her sentence.

Not talking to the woman ever again sounded like a fabulous idea, but I doubted I would be so lucky. As much as I would have loved to settle down and enjoy a quiet life in prison, I knew that wasn't an option for me. I had to get home to Phil.

And that would involve causing a little trouble.

After adjusting the machine back to 563.28 kelvin (the autoregulator was off), I scanned my surroundings until I found a window. A narrow pane next to the elevator afforded a beautiful view of the scenery—not that there was anything to see. The world outside was a blur of white and gray; it was impossible to tell where the cloudy sky ended and the snow-covered rocks began. The wind moaned as it tirelessly beat into the side of the building, like it was trying to bury us alive in a snowdrift.

I stared at the ice gathering in the corner of the window and calculated the odds. My last prison had been surrounded by the frigid north Atlantic, but swimming across the ocean would be a picnic compared to trekking down this mountain. I'd have better luck hacking into the elevator and riding down. But even if I could get to the bottom, what then? I'd have to hike back to civilization and beg for a ride to Beijing. All without going online, spending money, or revealing the fact that I was an escaped convict.

"All right, Jesus." I slapped my hand on the cold glass. "This is going to be exciting."

I thought you wanted a factory?

"Not a prison one," I reminded Him aloud. He went silent, so I closed the tab and brought my engineer's brain online.

Walking up to the railing, I surveyed the dazzling building and let my mind do its work. I began to see schematics, charts, and equations as my brain analyzed the laws of physics that made the enterprise run. It was a complicated machine—which meant there were a million ways to break it.

I grinned as I realized Asia had made her first fatal error. She never should have sent me to a place like this; the factory truly was a thing of beauty.

It would be such a pleasure to watch it burn.

11: PHILADELPHIA

The red *Record* button mocked me.

I glared at the sheet of remarks Jael had prepared. I was supposed to be making a statement about Nic. The publicity of his trial ensured that everybody—*everybody*—knew he was the anonymous "governor" I'd referred to in my videos, and my followers were demanding answers. But no matter how many times I paused the recording and tried again, I couldn't get the words out. It sounded like I was reading a eulogy—and in a way, I was.

Nic was gone. I knew he wasn't dead; Asia would have made a spectacle out of his execution. Instead, he'd been convicted with an absurd number of life sentences and sent to prison amidst the jeering of the media.

Of course, the location of his prison had been carefully omitted from the records. Jael, as always, claimed her people were on it, but so far, they had found nothing on or off the record indicating what had happened to him.

Jael finally told me I had to move on. Her team would keep searching, but in the meantime, I had a rebellion to lead—and my radio silence was causing rumors. So, she'd shut me in the recording studio with a list of soulless bullet points and ordered me to tell the world that I'd been orphaned for a second time.

Of course, I had to carefully omit the fact that it was all my fault.

No wonder it wasn't going well. It didn't help that they'd left me alone to stare at the merciless camera. I was in an office at the factory that had been converted into a recording studio, and the unnatural silence of the soundproofed space was claustrophobic. All I could hear was the rattling of my own grief as it beat into my chest like a whip. My breath was hot and shallow, and I ruined several takes by bursting into tears as I struggled to get the truth out.

I rubbed my eyes with the heels of my hands, ignoring the smear of mascara, and punched the button to restart the recording. Jael wouldn't let me out of this room until I recorded something usable.

Please, God, just help me get through this.

"Yes, Nic was an ally of mine," I droned. Maybe if I kept the emotion out of my voice, it would keep the feelings from crushing my lungs. "And his loss is my biggest regret. He shouldn't even have been on Earth, but he was trying to protect me—and now he's paid the ultimate price."

I shoved my notes aside with a grunt. I sounded just as bad as the liberal anchormen, blathering about platitudes that meant nothing. The truth was that Nic was in jail because I'd fought Asia and lost.

"I know you did this just to get back at me," I muttered at the camera. I probably shouldn't engage her, but I knew she was watching my streams. It was no secret what was going on between us.

"You did this because I didn't complete the mission, didn't you?" I gritted my teeth. "You thought I would give you your war, but I failed to perform, didn't I? I wasn't the gullible, obedient little daughter you needed me to be."

Suddenly, I could see her face, her narrow eyes glinting as she told me I was smart and beautiful and deserved to be a Nolan. She'd been grooming me, using flattery and makeup and gifts to cover up the evil in her heart. She had been luring me close—so she could murder what was most important to me.

And she succeeded.

A familiar heat ignited in my chest like flash paper. I lunged towards the camera, my voice rising to a shriek as I yelled at the one person who had caused all my pain.

"You monster! All this time, you claimed that you 'cared' about me, that you just wanted me to come home, that you wanted to be my friend. Well, those were all *lies*!"

I gripped the edge of the desk, afraid that if I didn't, I'd punch something. "You're a wicked, despicable woman, and people like you are the reason I hate the United. How do you sleep at night? You already took my dad away—wasn't that enough for you?"

I felt a burning behind my eyes and braced myself for the tears, but they never came. There was no more grief in my heart. All I could sense was a black, blinding rage.

"You took everything from me! You—"

I choked and slapped my hands over my mouth when I abruptly realized I was about to call her something much worse.

I stumbled back into the desk chair. *Oh God, I'm sorry, please forgive me.*

I dared to look at myself in the playback monitor. My face was so flushed and angry that it looked like I was about to murder someone with my bare hands. What had come over me? Had I really almost cussed someone out *on air*?

I couldn't do this anymore. I stabbed the button to stop the recording. At least we weren't live.

I stormed out of the studio and walked a few doors down to the conference room, where the others were meeting. Lanzhou, Bowen, and John and Dowe were all gathered around the head of the table with Jael, discussing whatever important memo was displayed on the projector. Well, Lanzhou and Bowen were getting work done; John and Dowe looked like they were doodling on a tablet.

Jael glanced up when the door whooshed open to announce my arrival. "Done for the day?"

"You're not going to be able to use the recording," I declared. I trudged up to the table and took the chair next to John and

Dowe, but only because they made a big show of pointing it out to me.

Jael raised an eyebrow. I sighed and twisted my hands in my lap. "I got upset and yelled at Asia. We probably shouldn't put that on air."

Jael shrugged. "Sounds like a video I'd watch."

I frowned at her. In her defense, I would probably watch that video too—and I wasn't sure that was a good thing.

"I don't know that we should engage the councilwoman head-on," Lanzhou cut in. "We don't want to antagonize her."

Jael's earrings flashed in the light as she propped her chin on her hand. "Everything Philadelphia says antagonizes Asia. That's why we have her on air."

The last thing I wanted was to be used as a cattle prod to provoke Asia, but I could tell that this conversation didn't involve me anymore.

"She's still the most powerful woman in China and arguably the United," Lanzhou insisted. "We already know this whole sham of a trial was to get revenge on Philadelphia. Don't you think that's enough collateral damage?"

Bowen shook his head and bounced his knee agitatedly. "No, I agree with Jael. I think we need to tell the whole world exactly who did it and why. Why are we not having Phil go on air and reveal everything she knows about Mong?"

I longed to tell the world who Asia really was, but Jael had forbidden it. I didn't have any evidence; I only knew what Nic had told me. To make matters worse, if I explained how I had met Asia, I would have to admit that my legal identity was Andromeda Nolan. And forfeiting Andromeda's clean file—and her money—was a sacrifice I knew Nic wouldn't want me to make.

"I need you to promise that you won't come for me. Promise me!"

"As much as I'd *love* to air that story," Jael said with gesture close to a smirk, "we need to focus on the operation. Asia isn't the real enemy—the United is."

"Respectfully, I disagree." Bowen stabbed the table with his finger. "This kind of behavior is precisely what makes the United evil. People need the truth, and if that means going to war against Mong, I say we do it."

"Except the person you're sending into battle is a teenage girl." Lanzhou at least had the decency to look in my direction as he talked about me like I wasn't in the room. "I don't like it. Philadelphia's suffered enough."

I opened my mouth, but Bowen was quicker to speak. "She's going to have to deal with her grief whether we air the story or not. She may as well use it to her advantage."

I glared at him. They were treating me like a paid actor, like my life's story was disposable propaganda for the rebellion. Did I not get a say in this?

"You make a good point," Jael agreed without the slightest bit of remorse. "Engagement goes up when she's vulnerable. It's part of why her videos trended in the first place—her pain is relatable."

I slapped my palms on the table. "My emotions are not clickbait!"

Everyone stopped and looked at me, and I flushed red.

Dowe jumped up to my defense. "That's right, they're not! Wait, what are we arguing about?"

"Dowe, please sit down," I groaned tiredly. He obeyed me with a shrug, but I felt a pinch in my chest. John and Dowe's antics had never bothered me before. What was wrong with me?

Jael frowned. "Do you need a break, Philadelphia?"

Probably, I thought but didn't say. What I needed was for this endless nightmare to be over.

"Because you look exhausted," she declared. If she was trying to be compassionate, she was failing to land the delivery.

Lanzhou leaned towards me. "Are you sleeping all right? We can get you medication for that."

I cringed at the thought. "I'm sleeping fine. I just cried a lot today." At least only half of that statement was a lie.

Jael studied me. "If you need a break, all you have to do is say something. If this is too much for you, I can send you back to Boston." The words were harsh, but her voice was too kind for it to be a threat. "We can do this remotely. I'll send John and Dowe with you."

"Road trip!" John cheered and went in for a high-five.

Dowe left him hanging. "Pretty sure we're going to have to fly."

I took a deep breath and tried to screw a lid back on my emotions. "No, I'm sorry, it's fine. I just—"

"No, I think that's a good idea," Lanzhou cut me off. He rose and faced Jael. "I really think she should go home. It's not safe here."

"Boston isn't exactly safe, either," Bowen argued. "And Mars is, regrettably, no longer an option."

I grimaced. He was right—there was no place for me on Mars anymore. My brother, Cea, and the rest of the residents had made it safely to the mining outpost, but it was so remote that Ephesus had difficulty getting a call through. It was only a temporary solution until we could figure out where to send them, and in the meantime, I couldn't even consult my brother for advice.

So much for keeping him involved.

Meanwhile, my friends in Boston weren't much better off. Stanyard had taken Ephesus's advice and convinced everyone to abandon the base. He'd sent his parents, his sister Mira, and my father to stay with friends, while he and a few others set up operations in another office building. Stanyard wouldn't tell me exactly where they were—just in case someone was listening to my calls.

"At least Boston is farther away from Councilwoman Mong." Lanzhou frowned at his cousin, a twinge of annoyance making it into his voice. "Look, we know the councilwoman did all of this to bait Philadelphia. Keeping her here is just tempting Mong to do something worse—and in the meantime, the entire Chinese surveillance state is helping track Philadelphia down. We'll have an advantage if we keep them apart and at least make the government work for it."

I swallowed as uncertainty gripped my chest. Everything Lanzhou was saying made sense—except it flew in the face of what God had promised me.

"I saw it all. You, in Beijing, as a Nolan, on even playing ground with Asia."

Bowen saw the same thing. "I disagree. Operation Blue Fire has twice as many followers here than it does in America, and this is where we need her most. If we can shake the government here, it will trickle down to other regions."

Jael drummed her acrylic nails on the table. "I tend to agree, as do the analytics on her videos."

"The analytics have nothing to do with where she records from," Lanzhou grunted. "I'd personally feel a lot better if she went home."

"Well, I wouldn't!" I raised my voice to be heard, desperate not to be left out of the conversation again. "I can't leave."

"Why not?" Lanzhou demanded, before checking the tone of his voice. He leaned on the table, eyes pleading with me. "Philadelphia, I promise you'll be just as effective from Boston as you would from—"

"Don't lie to her," Bowen snapped. "People will know if she leaves. It will weaken everything we've built here. Do you want to be responsible for that?"

Lanzhou folded his arms. "I don't want to be *responsible* for sacrificing a child."

"I'm not a child!" I protested, then realized I definitely sounded like one. I took a deep breath and tried to find the words that would make them understand. "Look, I won't leave until we find Nic."

"Philadelphia," Jael inserted, voice as smooth as unforgiving glass. "We've been over this. Nic is gone."

I felt the rage climb back up my throat. Why did everyone keep saying that? Nic was alive—I knew he was. Why was everyone else so quick to leave him for dead? Did he mean nothing to them?

Jael reached for my hand. "You need to let him go."

I jerked my wrist out of her grasp and shoved my chair back. "Well, I *can't!*"

It was only after the silence returned that I realized I was shouting again.

I winced. Since when had I become so angry? *This isn't like you.*

Jael shifted in her chair. "Philadelphia." It was a warning. "Are we going to have another incident?"

Shame flashed across my cheeks. "I'm sorry, I just…" I tried to lower my voice, but that just made me sound more pathetic, even to my ears. "I can't leave him, okay? He's like family, and besides, it's my fault he's in prison."

"No, Philadelphia, it isn't." Lanzhou's voice reached out to me, begging me to see his side. "You need to stop blaming yourself."

"Yes, it is! Do you know how many times he tried to get me to go back to Mars? He only came down here to save me, and he only got caught because of my *stupid chip.*"

No one denied it. I braced myself on the table and took a deep breath, trying and failing to find some clarity under the garbled emotions. "You're right," I admitted. "Asia is doing this because of me. And even now, I know that if I pick up the phone and call her, she'll tell me where he is. I could save him—I know I could. But he sacrificed himself for me, and now I have to just walk away and leave him for dead."

Tears stung my eyes. I tipped my head back and stared at the harsh fluorescents in the ceiling, hoping gravity would help me keep it together. "You have no idea what that feels like."

"Yes, I do."

I started and turned to Jael.

She wasn't looking at me. She picked up her tablet and swiped her fingers across the screen. The image on the projector changed to a cluttered dashboard of data and readouts.

"As an internet service provider, I control the algorithm on my network." Jael continued to narrate as she tabbed through submenus. "Every day, I get a new order from the government telling me what to censor and what to promote. I have to push the United's corrupted agenda—and suppress people and ideas I know are right."

She clicked a button, and a lengthy list of search terms appeared on the screen. She highlighted one and enlarged it so we could read it:

JEWISH GENOCIDE

I thought of Lev, the Russian teenager who worked for me back in Boston. He'd been orphaned by the government's attempt to purge America of race and religion. According to the statistics on Jael's screen, Brookline wasn't the only community the United had erased off the map.

I shivered and gripped my arms as a cold reminder prickled my skin. *This isn't about you.*

"I could fix this." Jael swiveled her chair to stare at the projection. "With one click, I could push this content to the front page and tell a third of the known world about the United's atrocities. I could end ignorance overnight. But I only get one chance before the government catches me and takes my job away." She tapped the tablet, and the projection went dark.

I stared at the bland wall where the image had been. She was right; she did understand how I felt. It would be maddening to know that I had the power to change everything but couldn't— and in the meantime, I was the primary weapon the United was using to enforce their rule.

"That's why I chose you."

I jerked out of my daze as she turned back to face me. She folded her hands on the table and leaned over to get in my line of vision. "I know exactly how you're feeling, and I can't promise that it will get any better. You're going to have to live with the weight of your decisions, and every day you're going to wake up, look in the mirror, and wonder who you've become. That's why you have to center your gravity on what you know is right, not on your feelings."

I let the tears fall. I already had that center. Even Nic knew what I had to do.

"Don't ever come back."

Jael found my hand. "So, I'll ask you again, Blue Fire: Can you handle this?"

12: PHILADELPHIA

It was almost five o'clock by the time we left the conference room.

"Who's ready for church? Besides me!" John cheered. He jumped up and slapped the doorframe with an agility that was terrifying for his age.

Dowe jostled my shoulder. "Race you to the cafeteria." He took off without waiting for an answer. John hollered and bolted after him, waving both arms above his head like an inflatable.

Bowen chuckled. "Yes, you should come with us." He encouraged me with a smile and started walking towards the elevator at a much calmer pace.

I forced myself to return the smile as I followed him. Being crammed in a room with hundreds of people—most of whom thought I was a war hero—sounded closer to hell than heaven, but I knew church was the best place for me.

Lanzhou picked up the rear as we descended into the basement of the factory. The Tangs hosted nightly services in the company cafeteria, where shift change concealed the flow of people in and out of the building. Several off-duty workers greeted me by name as we walked past the lockers and down the back hallway that led to the podium.

The thrum of chatter and prayer vibrated in the corridor, like a giant engine was rumbling in the walls. I peered around the corner and saw that the cafeteria was packed. You could barely see the stained plastic tables amongst the throng of excited worshippers. Had there been that many people the last time I visited?

Bowen unwittingly answered my question. "Attendance has nearly doubled since you started coming," he explained with a grin.

I felt a pressure form in my chest and tried to decide if it was joy or anxiety. "Won't that raise suspicion?" The Tangs had been hosting this church for over ten years without incident, but surely the government would notice if an extra thousand people started visiting the factory every night.

Lanzhou didn't seem concerned. "I might have to slip a little extra to my contact at the police station, but I'm not going to turn away hungry souls."

"Besides, people feel safe when you're here." Bowen grabbed a microphone off a stand and checked the battery.

I stared at him. "They do?"

Instead of answering, he handed me the microphone. "Will you come on stage with us?"

All my panic lodged in my throat as the weight of the microphone settled in my hands like a dead body. I was the last person who should be on stage. I was emotional and sleep-deprived, and I hadn't heard from God in what felt like years. But I didn't want to admit that in so many words, so instead I stuttered, "I-I don't know what to say."

"Then don't say anything." Bowen pressed his thumb to a locked cabinet door. It beeped and popped open, revealing a stack of contraband Bibles. "Just worship. That's what people really need to see."

He made it sound so simple, but I wasn't sure I had the soul to put on a show tonight. All I wanted to do was curl up on the floor at the altar and beg God for mercy. I needed the worship to carry *me*—how could I carry someone else?

"What do I do?" I asked the question aloud, but I wasn't really talking to any of them.

Bowen's expression softened, and I could see that the revolutionary had been replaced by the pastor. "What is the Spirit asking you to do?"

Nothing. I searched my soul, but there was only dark, cavernous silence.

Just like there had been for weeks.

Bowen laid his hand on my shoulder. "Remember, worship isn't about feelings—it's about obedience. If you don't hear anything, do what you know you should do, and the rest will catch up."

Lanzhou joined the conversation. "Your mind, will, and emotions are yours to control. So, tell them what to do." He reached into a closet and pulled out a suit jacket. "'Why, my soul, are you downcast?'"

"You want a list?" I muttered, and too late realized I'd used real words.

Lanzhou winked as he shrugged on the jacket. "David also had a lot to complain about—but he wrote a whole psalm telling himself what to do."

"'Praise the Lord, my soul, and forget not all his benefits'!" Bowen echoed, his voice tripping on the edge of song. He guided me gently towards the stairs that led to the podium. "You don't have to use the microphone if you don't want to. Just help me show the people what kind of God we serve."

I instinctively followed him onto the stage, even though I couldn't remember making a conscious decision to move. I felt the shift in the crowd—the excited murmurs as the center of attention tipped to one side—as soon as I walked onto the platform. I forced a pretty smile, the same one I put on for the camera, and avoided looking anyone in the eye.

Bowen took center stage and greeted the crowd in Mandarin. He was repaid with cheers and shouts, the only word of which I understood was "Amen." Lanzhou then took over, pacing back and forth as he read from his Bible. I listened politely to the foreign words and fidgeted with the jade bangle around my wrist. The jewelry had been given to me by this very congregation as a reminder that they were interceding for my protection. I'd barely taken it off since, and I could only hope they were still praying for me.

Because at the moment, I didn't even know how to pray for myself.

Another leader I didn't recognize struck up an a cappella song. Almost everyone was singing in Mandarin, so I turned my microphone off and did just what Bowen suggested: I went through the motions. I sang along in tongues, I bowed when everyone else bowed, and I raised my hands when anyone took the stage to pray. I did everything I knew how to do and threw my whole body into it, desperate to feel anything besides confusion and fear.

I never did. I slipped into the rhythm of the service and participated along with everybody else, but all my actions felt empty. I'm sure I looked holy and passionate to an observer, but I knew I wasn't there, no matter how much I wanted to be. It was like my body wasn't even mine anymore.

I knew what it felt like to lose control to the Holy Spirit. This wasn't it.

This was death.

*

It was 3am, and I was nowhere near sleeping.

Even Tommy had given up on me. Annoyed by my constant tossing and turning, he'd vacated the bed and claimed a spot on the windowsill. With the shutters closed, the ledge was incredibly narrow; half his legs dangled off, and he looked like he could end up on the floor at any moment. But apparently that was still preferable to lying next to me.

I didn't blame him. Every few minutes, I flipped over, contorting this way and that, searching for the center of gravity that would make it all go away. But as soon as I laid still, as soon as I stopped rustling on the sheets, the silence came back, and with it the keen knowledge that my heart was racing. I could practically hear my thoughts echoing in the room as they whipped around and around without purpose.

I finally gave up and turned the bedside lamp on. If I was going to lie awake, I might as well read. At least then my mind would be filled with something other than unanswered questions.

I grabbed my backpack and pulled out the paper Bible Stanyard had given me. It was a vintage black leather-bound volume, one of the most beautiful—and illegal—things I owned.

I fingered the slight water damage on the corner. I hadn't spent much time reading the Bible lately—maybe that was my problem.

Propping myself on the pillows, I opened the book to a random page. I flipped through my favorite passages, searching for inspiration. Eventually, I landed on the chapter with my name on it, as I often did.

"See, I have placed before you an open door that no one can shut."

I sighed and tapped the page. *I sure don't feel like any doors are opening for me right now, God.*

Before I could wait for an answer, my tablet pinged. I knew without looking who it was: Stanyard.

It had been incredibly hard to hide my insomnia from him, if only because the time difference meant I was awake when he was online and working. I knew I should tell him what was going on; he'd want to know. But I was so afraid that if anyone found out I wasn't sleeping, the Tangs would put me back on medication, and then I wouldn't have control over my life—or my actions—anymore. So, I'd kept my mouth shut and avoided reading Stanyard's messages late at night so he wouldn't know I was awake.

He'd been busy today; this was probably the fifth time he'd messaged me. I set my Bible on the bedspread and took my tablet off its charger. I couldn't open the app, or he would know I'd read his messages. I also couldn't turn off that feature; I knew I'd get a lecture about it. Instead, I swiped through the previews on my home screen.

FINALLY FINISHED DECRYPTING THE CODE ON YOUR CHIP. YOU WERE RIGHT—THERE'S TWO SETS OF DNA ON HERE.

I chewed my lip. In some weird way, I was relieved to know that my chip *had* been coded to kill the General Secretary. At least I didn't go through all the pain and terror of resisting Jayde for nothing.

But that also meant I was right about everything else: Someone was trying to kill Nic.

But who? A flip through the rest of Stanyard's messages confirmed we weren't any closer to answering that question.

IF IT WAS DATA, HE CLEARLY DIDN'T TELL JAYDE. I CAN FIND ABSOLUTELY NO EVIDENCE ON THE SERVER THAT JAYDE HAD ANY IDEA WHAT WAS GOING ON. IN FACT, I DON'T THINK ANYONE ON BASE KNEW ABOUT IT.

THE ONLY TIME NIC IS MENTIONED IN THE LAST MONTH IS WHEN I CALLED HIM.

I remembered. Jayde and I had been deep in planning the assassination. It was a blackout mission, so I couldn't even talk to Stanyard. I'd spent all my time in the shooting range, training to kill. Stanyard saw I was on a downward spiral and alerted Nic.

THERE'S A RECORD OF THE CALL BECAUSE I MADE IT FROM BASE, AND JAYDE MUST HAVE SEEN IT. HE TEXTED DATA AND A FEW OTHERS.

The message was followed by a screenshot. The text in the thumbnail was too small to read, but I knew what had happened. Jayde had realized that Stanyard was trying to talk me out of the mission. He knew Stanyard was a threat; that's why he used him as blackmail. No wonder he'd been watching the security cameras in the range the next day and saw when Stanyard and I kissed.

I pinched my tablet until the screen flashed up a warning. *We should have been more careful.*

I forced my fingers to relax and scrolled to Stanyard's last message.

I'LL KEEP DIGGING. THIS DOESN'T COMPLETELY RULE OUT THAT DATA IS INVOLVED—BUT IT'S NOT LOOKING LIKELY. EVERYTHING I'VE FOUND FROM DATA SUGGESTS HE SUPPORTS YOU. HE EVEN BLACKLISTED JAYDE AND REVOKED HIS ACCESS CODES AFTER JAYDE KIDNAPPED YOU.

I read the last sentence a second time. The fact that Data hated Jayde didn't necessarily mean he could be trusted—but it was certainly a point in his favor.

I tossed the tablet on the bed and buried my chin in a pillow. Some of my anxiety drifted away, leaving confusion in its place. Stanyard was right; just because there was no activity on the base's server didn't mean anything. Data—or even Jayde—could have been smart and avoided talking about it while they were on base. But seeing as there was a bunch of other sensitive information on the server—including, apparently, the fact that Jayde had been planning to hold Stanyard hostage—that didn't seem likely. Since neither Data nor Jayde had an obvious motive for killing Nic, I was beginning to favor the simple solution: It wasn't anyone on base.

But if Jayde and Data didn't want Nic dead, then who did?

Another message came through. I tapped the screen and read the notification.

CALL ME WHEN YOU GET UP. THERE'S SOMEONE WHO WANTS TO TALK TO YOU.

He followed it with a smiling emoji, which I found mildly horrifying. Stanyard *never* used emojis. How was I supposed to interpret that? Was that a good sign or a bad sign?

Curiosity overcame my resolve. I wasn't in any danger of sleeping anyway.

After putting on a sweater and smoothing my hair, I opened the app and dialed Stanyard.

He answered immediately. "Phil! What are you doing up? My texts didn't wake you, did they?"

"No," I begrudgingly admitted. "I couldn't sleep."

His video connected. He squinted at the camera, but my face was half in shadow thanks to the soft light of the bedside lamp. Hopefully that meant he couldn't see how bloodshot my eyes were.

"How long has this been going on?" he prompted.

I shrugged dismissively. "It's no big deal—"

"Phil," he cut me off, but not unkindly. "You promised."

I flinched. He was right—I did promise. And if I couldn't trust him with something as simple as this, how could I trust him with anything else?

"You say you trust me. So, start trusting me with things."

"About two weeks," I confessed.

"Why didn't you tell me sooner?"

I avoided his eyes. "Because I was afraid that if I told anyone, the Tangs would try to put me back on medication. I can't take any more pills." I swallowed the shame and forced the truth out. "I don't trust myself on medication—not after what happened."

I braced myself for the disappointment, but it never came. "Thank you for telling me how you feel," he said gently. "I'll talk to Mrs. Nolan. Surely there's something else you can do besides medication."

According to the government, Mrs. Nolan was Andromeda's mother. We'd never been family, but I did trust her—and she was a nurse. If anyone would know what to do, it was her.

I looked back into the camera. "Thank you." I took a breath and was surprised to find that my chest didn't feel as tight.

You can trust him.

Stanyard sealed the deal with a warm smile. "Since you're awake... are you up to talking to someone?"

"Yeah, that's why I called. What's with the emoji? Are you feeling okay?"

He chuckled and stood up. "You'll see. It's good news, I promise."

The camera swung to a view of the ceiling as he started walking. I watched the fluorescent lights flash by and tried to match his anticipation. Who would want to talk to me, and why didn't they just call me themselves?

A door opened. "Hey," Stanyard greeted someone off-screen. "She's actually awake, so if you're up to talking now..."

The other person must have nodded an affirmative, because the camera jerked again as the device was handed off. The stranger waited until Stanyard had left and shut the door, then lifted the camera to his face. I sucked in my breath.

Dad.

13: PHILADELPHIA

My father looked exactly as he had on the day we'd been separated. You couldn't tell he'd been frozen and revived—if anything, he looked *too* young, the freshly-regenerated skin replacing the wrinkles that should have been there. But his hair was still feathered with a tired gray, and his eyes were still framed with crow's feet that weren't quite happy as he gazed at me with an unreadable expression.

I stared back, unable to formulate words. It had been over two months since I'd spoken to my dad, and suddenly, I was afraid to. There was so much I needed to say, but all the words felt trapped underneath the apology it was too late to give, like water at the bottom of a freezing lake.

To my surprise, he initiated. "Philadelphia?"

I gasped. "You-you know who I am? But how—"

He raised a hand, as if to pause my racing heart. "Stanyard has been telling me all about you—about us."

"He has?" My breath caught in my throat again, but this time, it wasn't a painful feeling.

My dad nodded. "He's visited me every day and told me stories, showed me pictures... He repeats everything multiple times and makes me recite it back to him. It's like being in, ah..." He hesitated, like the chip in his brain was struggling to find the word. "...School."

I could picture the scene—and realized, perhaps for the first time, just how much Stanyard loved me.

"I wish I could say I remembered it for myself." My dad sighed, and doubt flickered across his expression like lightning behind a cloud. "But from what he's described, you sound like an..." he searched for the words, "...intelligent, courageous young woman, and I should be proud to have you as a daughter."

I blinked away warm tears. "He may have embellished my resume slightly. Did he... tell you about what's going on between us?"

Dad squinted at the camera. "What about you two?"

Heat crawled across my cheeks, and I could see in the playback monitor that I had turned bright red. Why was it so embarrassing to say it out loud? Literally everybody else knew about it.

"Is there something I should know?"

My father arched one eyebrow—and I burst out laughing. The gesture was too cute to be stern, and I abruptly realized just how much I had missed this.

"Stanyard and I are dating," I managed after I swallowed my giggles. "And, I guess after all that's happened, I never expected to be talking to my dad about boys."

"That does explain a lot," my father admitted with something close to a smile. "I'm afraid I don't know enough about either of you yet to give an opinion, but from what I've seen of him, he seems like a good man."

"He is." I sank back against the pillows, letting the silence of the quiet night return. I wanted to float away on this feeling—this sense that, for the first time in a long time, something was right in the world. Asia had taken a lot from me this week, but I hadn't lost everything.

Thank you, Jesus.

Dad seemed uncomfortable with the lull in conversation, so I sat back up. "How are you feeling?"

"I've only got a couple weeks' experience to compare it to," he grunted with a morbid attempt at humor, "but better."

"And your... mind?" I wasn't sure what I was asking, but I wanted to know everything.

"I'd be lying if I said it wasn't frustrating that everyone expects me to have fifty years of life experience when I can only remember the last three weeks," he snapped.

I cringed. "I'm sorry, we don't have to talk about it."

"No, I'm sorry. I'm just tired." He rubbed his head self-consciously. "I know everyone's trying to help, and they tell me it's working."

I swallowed when I remembered who "they" were. "I heard Data helped you with your speech," I said, parsing my words slowly to keep the suspicion out of them.

My dad nodded. "It was dis... disorienting at first—to go from not being able to find the words for anything to suddenly knowing a dictionary. But it really did help."

I picked at the bedspread. "Has he been taking good care of you?"

"He's nice. I haven't seen him much this week," Dad commented, unbothered. "It's been... the big guy with the tattoos?"

I helped him out. "Andes." Andes was a Scotsman who, like Seoul, was willing to perform all kinds of procedures outside the law. He'd done my tattoo and implanted the wiring for my chip, and he'd overseen my dad's revival.

"Yeah, him. They said they're going to try and help me recover my science degrees next. If a chip can expand my vocabulary, maybe it can teach me chemistry, too." He flicked his finger against his temple like one might kick a delinquent vending machine.

I stiffened. *If Seoul can get me one of those memory devices, I can bring all of you back.*

"It won't be the same as if I learned it from scratch, but maybe if I start doing it, muscle memory will kick in. I don't know." He groaned, and for a second, I could see all of the hopelessness and pain clouding his expression. "I just wish I could remember some of this for myself."

I pinched my eyes shut. How I wanted to tell him that it might be possible, that we might be able to recover what he lost.

But I knew I shouldn't get his hopes up until I had the device in my hand. The last I'd heard from Seoul was that she had a lead, but she still didn't have a timeline—or a price.

Please, God. Grant me favor.

"Just like I wish I could remember you."

I looked back down at the screen. My father's face had softened as he studied me. I realized, in his mind, he was seeing his daughter for the first time. I brushed my bleached hair behind my ears and wished I could be the girl he'd left behind.

"I want… I want to talk with you more." His voice tripped as he struggled to overcome the barrier between us. "I want to get to know you again. If I can."

"Of course, Dad," I whispered, fighting tears. "I'll call as often as you want."

He frowned. "Are you not coming back to Boston?"

I stiffened. "Did someone say I was?"

"No, I just assumed you were." He visibly leaned way from the screen. "Your family is here, after all."

"I'm sorry, I didn't mean it like that." I tried to shove past the doubts that cluttered my mind like books upended off a case. "But I can't leave Nic behind."

"Who?"

"Nic, my…" *My other parent.* "The man who came over to China with me."

"Oh, him." My father's eyes darkened. "I don't think you should wait for him. He's not your responsibility." He said it flippantly, callously—just like everyone else I'd talked to today.

"I have to! It's my fault, okay?" I shouted, and then caught myself too late.

My father flinched and looked confused, like a dog that had been kicked for no reason. I glanced away as shame burned behind my ears. I was probably the first person to yell at him since he woke up.

"I'm sorry, I shouldn't have shouted," I whispered. "It's just… everyone keeps telling me I should leave him behind. But I *can't.*"

"Why not?" This time, the question was gentle.

Because it's not supposed to be this way. This wasn't right—I knew it wasn't. God didn't bring Nic back to life just to kill him again, and He didn't drag both of us to China without a reason. We had a purpose for being here. I couldn't give up on that—I *wouldn't* give up on that. I was supposed to be in Beijing, even if no one else but Nic could see that.

But I couldn't explain all that to my father. He was confused enough already; listening to me rant about an open vision some strange man had about me would push him over the edge. So instead, I told him the other half of the truth: "I can't leave him behind because he didn't leave me behind."

My father seemed to accept that answer. He nursed the silence for a minute before responding. "Look, I don't know this man, and from what little I've heard, I'm not sure I like him."

I chuckled as the air came back into the room. I'd feel the same way if I'd only gotten the synopsis of Nic's life. "There's another half to the story. I'll tell you, when you're ready."

My dad acknowledged the offer with a half-smile. "But I've heard a *lot* about you, and if everything they're saying is true, then I know you won't give up."

I focused on his face again. He shifted in his chair and leaned towards the camera, closing the gap he'd created. "To hear Stanyard tell it, you don't give up on anything or anyone. You keep fighting even when you know you'll lose. That's why they picked you to be... what is it again? 'Blue Fire'?"

I gripped the tablet as my father's words muddled with Jael's in my mind.

"I only get one chance. That's why I chose you."

"I won't pretend that I understand anything that's going on," my dad admitted, "but if this man means that much to you, then you should fight for him. Just like you fought for me."

He offered a sad smile. I returned it, not bothering to stop the tears this time. "Thanks, Dad. I love you."

"Give me some time," he murmured, choking on his own tears, "and I think I'll be able to say the same thing about you."

The light in the room behind him shifted as a door opened off-screen. "Thomas, are you—oh, sorry, didn't know you were on a call."

"Tower!" I called, recognizing my uncle's voice.

My dad looked up at his brother-in-law as he walked into frame. "'Tower'?" he questioned.

"Old codename. You used to be Catalyst." Tower clapped my father on the shoulder and greeted me with a nod. "Good to see you, Phil. I won't interrupt."

My father started to rise. "No, that's okay."

I could tell he was exhausted from the conversation, so I gave him an out. "I actually want to talk to Tower—I mean, Uncle Bart, if that's okay."

Dad nodded gratefully and handed the tablet over to Tower. My uncle waited until my father had walked away and the door had shut behind him before claiming the vacant chair. "'Uncle Bart,' eh? Sounds weird coming from you," he chided.

I had to agree. Tower had been estranged for most of my life, and it wasn't until several months after I met him that he decided to admit we were related. Mom's death—a tragedy my dad was partly responsible for—had made everything more complicated than it should have been. "We can stick with Tower. You two seem to be getting along, though," I noted with a twinge of happiness.

"I think he likes me better now that he can't remember me." My uncle smiled, but I could tell the gesture didn't make it to his sunken eyes.

"Thanks for taking care of him," I offered.

"We'll always be family, Phil," he deferred. "But that's not what we need to talk about it, is it?"

I sighed. "No, it's not."

He mercifully took the lead. "Heard you met Jael."

"Yeah. When were you going to tell me?" I accused, even as I wondered how many times I'd have to open conversations with my uncle like this. Tower had met Jael several months ago. They'd both known about the assassination plot, and they'd mutually agreed to send me to Beijing with Jayde. John and Dowe, Jael's agents, were supposed to intercept me before I got to the General.

That plan had failed miserably, but I didn't blame Jael or Tower for John and Dowe's mistakes. What I wanted to know was why my uncle had seen fit to send me on a suicide run without telling me.

Tower shook his head listlessly, as if he didn't know the answer to that question either. "I didn't trust Jayde. I had no idea how many allies he had, and I didn't want you to get hurt."

That wasn't the first time I'd heard that excuse, but it didn't hold water. "You literally drove me home the night before we left. If you were worried about my safety, you could have gotten me out of town."

Of course, it wouldn't have been the first time my uncle had the power to get me to safety—but didn't.

He stared at me long and hard from somewhere under his mop of disobedient hair. "If you want the boring answer, I was just following orders. Jael wanted you in Beijing. She knew you would be more effective there than in Boston."

I sighed. My uncle wasn't telling me anything I didn't already know—I was here because Jael was in control.

"And I agreed with her."

I looked back down at the screen. "Then you think I should be here?"

"Still do," he consented without emotion.

I tapped my fingers on the back of my tablet nervously. "Everyone else thinks I should come home. They say it's not safe here."

"'Everyone else' doesn't know how to fight a war," he returned. "And no, it's not safe. I didn't send you to Beijing because I thought it was safe. I sent you to Beijing because I knew you could win."

I swallowed as my heart started thrumming in the back of my throat. Maybe Nic wasn't the only person who saw the truth.

Tower leaned towards the camera, his posture conveying the urgency his drawling voice did not. "This is war, Phil. I'm not your uncle—I'm your ally. And if you're going to survive out there, you need to start thinking of the world in those terms."

I had to admit that this whole ordeal would have been a lot easier had I not expected Tower to act like family. Maybe that was why he never wanted to tell me we were related.

"You need to pick your battles and fight to win," he continued sternly. "There are people—like your boyfriend—who aren't going to agree with your decisions. But you're not a civilian anymore, and you can't afford to think like one."

I glanced at the bedside table, where I'd abandoned my wig and hair clip earlier in the evening. The feather glowed a dull blue in the diffused light of the lamp. Was that what I was now—a soldier?

"So yes, I think you should stay in Beijing." Tower settled back in the chair, as if he'd done his duty and was clocking out. "But I'm not your commanding officer. Jael is."

With a familiar check in my spirit, I remembered that she wasn't my only "commanding officer." I answered to Someone Else—and He had made it explicitly clear that He wanted me in China.

"So, what are your orders, Blue Fire?" my uncle prodded.

"'Wake the people up,'" I recited. That's what Jael was always saying, but I realized, as soon as the words left my mouth, that she wasn't the only one speaking it over me.

Wake My people up.

I dropped the tablet in my lap and gripped the bedspread with both hands. Suddenly, I knew what God was saying. I couldn't explain how I knew. I hadn't heard a voice, but the knowledge was so overwhelming that it was like a concrete object I could hold. I felt the pressure in my chest and the motion in the Spirit that told me it was the Lord.

I glanced at my open Bible. With my finger, I traced back a few verses to the letter to the church in Sardis:

"Wake up! Strengthen what remains and is about to die, for I have found your deeds unfinished in the sight of my God. Remember, therefore, what you have received and heard; hold it fast, and repent. But if you do not wake up, I will come like a thief, and you will not know at what time I will come to you."

I pressed my palm flat on the book. *This* was my purpose. This was why I was here. This was why Blue Fire existed.

Because it was time to wake up.

"There she is," my uncle chuckled, and for the first time, some joy made it into his voice. "I can see it in your eyes—you figured it out."

I blinked as the room came back into focus. "Yeah, I guess so."

"Glad to be of assistance. Now, how can I help you succeed, lieutenant?"

He said it with a wink, but I knew he was serious. Only trouble was, I had no idea how to answer him. How *could* he help? How could anyone help? Of course, he could promote my videos, but everyone did that. There had to be something more that he could do—there had to be something more that *I* could do.

Tommy finally decided to join me on the bed. He jumped up in my lap and flicked his tail against my chin, demanding attention. I absentmindedly stroked him as I let the thoughts churn over in my mind.

If this was my calling, then I wanted to do more. Spamming the internet with propaganda videos would only go so far, and Operation Blue Fire was a little over a month away. We needed more people and more support. I couldn't just sit back in my glitzy recording studio and hope everything turned out all right. There had to be more to Blue Fire than looking pretty in front of a camera.

I stiffened as Bowen's words came rolling back to me.

"Attendance has nearly doubled since you started coming. People feel safe when you're here."

"What is it?" Tower prodded.

I pushed Tommy aside and picked up the tablet. "I have an idea."

14: NIC

"Q, I thought we had an agreement never to speak to each other again," Warden Ivanova cooed as she perched on the edge of her desk.

I gestured with cuffed hands. "In my defense, if my plan had worked, we *wouldn't* be talking."

Regrettably, Warden Ivanova and I had gotten thoroughly acquainted over the past week. My attempts to escape had ensured that we'd talked almost daily.

The first few infractions were minor; I was mainly gathering data on the effectiveness of their security systems. But yesterday I'd tried to hack the controls on the elevator that led out of the complex. When that failed, I'd attempted to break into the maintenance shaft and hitch a ride down. That had also failed, and after they'd dredged me out of the bottom of the maintenance shaft (I don't want to talk about it), they hauled me straight to the warden's office.

"As much as I'm enjoying our chats, I really don't have time to entertain your repeated stupidity." She sighed and contemplated the contents of her mug.

"Neither do I, frankly." I drummed my fingers on my knees and wondered what deterrent she'd try this time. The fact that they'd dragged me to her office made me hopeful that I wouldn't be thrown over the railing, at least.

"Unfortunately," she slammed her mug down on the desk, "you don't seem to be motivated by pain, and I'm under strict orders from Mong not to kill you intentionally."

I filled in the blanks. "But accidents do happen."

"Frequently," she admitted. "But you've only been here, what, a week? That's a bit early for me to be losing my patience. I don't think she'll buy that story."

"Regrettably for both of us, you're probably right." I had no doubts Asia was keeping me alive like an ace in her back pocket, and that, weirdly, would be my saving grace. "So, same time tomorrow?"

"I'll clear my afternoon." Warden Ivanova jumped off the desk. "But factor this into your calculations, Q: Whatever Mong wants you for, it has an expiration. As soon as she's done with you, if you haven't fallen in line, I'll be collecting my vengeance with interest."

"Noted. Moving on, what are you feeling like today?" I hoped whatever torture she picked was short; I had to get back to my cell and plan for tomorrow.

"Honestly, Q, I've had a bad day," she whined, like we were friends commiserating over coffee. She walked over to the wall and surveyed the weapons she had hanging there. "Production is down, and the big boss docked my pay."

"That does sound terrible," I admitted. "Do you need to talk about it?"

"I think a nice, old-fashioned beating would relieve the stress, if you're offering." She yanked a baton off its hook and turned to me.

"Happy to be of service," I grunted, and braced myself.

*

The beating did wonders, and by the time Warden Ivanova was finished with me, her mood had turned completely around. She was so grateful for my help that she told me to take the rest of the week off.

I spent the first forty-eight hours of my vacation in the infirmary, getting my bones put back together, and the remaining seventy-two locked in solitary confinement. The privacy was welcome; I needed to rework my escape plans.

There was only one problem: My plans didn't need to be reworked.

The more I ran the simulations in my mind, the more I realized there was nothing wrong with my theories. My calculations were flawless, as they always were. I had spent every waking hour cataloging how this prison was run. I had memorized the guards' rotations, the prisoners' shifts, and the timing of deliveries. I knew exactly where everyone was supposed to be at any given moment, and I could tamper with every machine in a dozen ways. There was absolutely no logical reason one or more of my attempts shouldn't have succeeded.

And yet, all of my plans had failed for the most inane reasons. The first time, my wrench broke. The second time, the guard who was supposed to be on shift overslept. The third time—when I'd tried to break into the elevator shaft—we had the warmest temperatures on record (which is saying something when you're 20,000 feet in the air). That threw off the pressure in the shaft and caused the maintenance hatch to stick.

As a scientist, I was always prepared for unexpected variables. But this was too ridiculous to be coincidental. The fact that they'd recorded a double-digit temperature for the first time in a hundred years made me wonder if something—or Someone—didn't want me to escape.

"Look," I said, breaking the silence in my cold cell, "I could use Your help with this."

There was no response. He hadn't said much for the past week. And even though I got way more done when I was the only one talking, I was smart enough to know that silence in the Spirit was rarely a good sign.

"Let me rephrase." I took a deep breath to filter the frustration out of my tone. "I *need* Your help with this. I can't do this without You."

That must have been one of His favorite phrases, because He responded immediately.

You didn't ask Me if I wanted you to leave.

I shot a glare at the corner of the room next to the door, because that's where I'd decided, arbitrarily, that He was standing. "I thought it was implied. In case You forgot, the teenager *You* told me to take care of is stranded by herself *in China*, and she's trying to lead a revolution. And, unless there was a typo in that vision You sent me, You wanted me to help her."

I don't do typos.

"Exactly. So, I think our highest priority should be getting me out of jail."

It's certainly your highest priority.

I heard the pause—that breath of air that told me God was about to leave the chat and let me simmer in my own thoughts—and realized what He was implying.

"What? You really want me to stay here and freeze while she's out there alone?"

He would have arched an eyebrow had He had one. I stood up and gestured broadly at the corner.

"That's Your endgame? Leave me to rot in prison while she fights and dies in a war she doesn't understand?"

And what if it is?

"Then we have a problem."

There was silence—one opportunity for me to repent.

Then He took the cue and left, leaving the room colder than before.

I shivered in solitary for another twelve hours, and then they finally decided I could play with the other kids again. I sulked down to mess hall to get my first hot meal in five days.

I walked into the cafeteria and was alarmed to find that the place was packed. A rough calculation told me there were 37%

more workers crammed in the greasy room than usual, which could only mean one thing: They'd served two shifts at the same time. That never happened.

I tried to swallow the rock that spawned in my stomach. *What are You up to?*

I was a little surprised when He responded. *I thought you were hungry.*

I was actually considering starting a forty-day fast. I already have a three-day head start.

I didn't ask you to fast. Get in there.

The inmate behind me in line encouraged me with his elbows, so I obeyed begrudgingly. I grabbed my rations and then wandered around the room for ten minutes, looking for an empty table. There wasn't one, so I chose the lesser of two evils and picked a table with only two people at it.

I realized I'd made a mistake when one of them saw me approach and started waving.

"*Hola*, Q!"

I halted a safe distance away. "Do I know you?"

"No, but everyone heard about your stunt in the maintenance shaft. Is it true they had to use old cooking grease to get you loose?" The little man propped his elbows on the table and waited eagerly for my answer.

"It was clean oil," I mumbled. "And the pressure in the shaft was off."

The other man at the table spoke up. "That's because the insulation in that corridor is not up to code." His heavy German accent made the words so thick they dragged on the floor. "They should be using insulation with an R-value of at least 80, but I'm pretty sure that shaft has R-60, at best."

"It looked like R-55 to me," I started, then caught myself. "Wait, who are you, again?"

"Oh, my apologies. I'm Vance." He nodded his head.

"Ryan!" the other guy volunteered. "You going to sit down or what?"

I did so hesitantly, studying them from across the table. The two were so proportionately imbalanced that it was a wonder the bench didn't tip over. Vance was so big and hulking that if he claimed to be three full-size men in a trench coat, I would have believed him. Every square inch of him was packed with dense muscles, and cruel scars decorated his face and hands like battle trophies. His dirty blond hair shadowed his stonewalled face as he hunched over the table, like he was a giant who condescended to live with us mere mortals.

Ryan, on the other hand, had to stretch every vertebra in his spine to be seen over the edge of the table. He was a compact man who acted like a windup toy whose gear and been cranked one too many times. All his motions were broad and dramatic, like he constantly overshot how far he had to move his limbs. He was investing way too much energy into everything, including breathing; I was getting exhausted just watching him, and I had only been blessed by his presence for sixty seconds.

"Whatcha in for, Q?" he chirped. His voice was about seventeen pitches too high for my comfort, and his perky Hispanic accent wasn't helping.

"Breaking my girlfriend's heart," I deadpanned, which wasn't entirely inaccurate. "You?"

"Domestic terrorism," he replied around a mouthful of food. "Apparently I organized an incredibly successful riot in Shanghai."

I knew better than to ask, but I was a glutton for punishment. "'Apparently'?" I prodded.

He scratched the back of his neck like an anxious dog. "Yeah, so, I was *trying* to organize a demonstration in San Antonio. But I outsourced the distribution of the pamphlets to this Chinese factory, and apparently there was a miscommunication, because the papers got printed in Mandarin instead of Spanish…"

"That's what you get for not supporting American jobs," Vance grunted.

Ryan shrugged and made a drawn-out "aye" sound, punctuated with a flap of his hands. "So, I'm not exactly sure what I organized, but it was very successful—enough that they extradited me here."

A random prisoner walking by our table must have overheard the comment, because he stopped and declared, "Best riot ever!" He offered Ryan a high-five, which he returned, although he practically had to stand on the bench to reach it.

I guess Philadelphia isn't the only one guilty of accidental terrorism, I thought, and then paused when the memory made me unduly sad.

Ryan sat back down and turned to me with a grin. "People keep telling me I should organize another one. I don't know if you'd be interested in something like that—you reckon you'd be interested?"

"No, but I know someone I can pass your information along to," I returned. I leaned back on the bench so I could look up at Vance. "And what's your story?" I figured I might as well get all the annoying pleasantries out of the way now, so if we were unfortunate enough to meet again, we could spare ourselves the misery of small talk.

He laid his fork down and cleared his throat. "It's quite complicated..."

"Sorry I asked," I muttered.

He kept going. "In fact, had I reported the numbers differently, what I did would not have been considered a crime in most jurisdictions. But in the United's Consolidated Tax Code, there's a subset of ordinance 1023(c)4 that states—"

"You lost me at 'subset,'" I cut him off. "In stupid people's terms, please?"

He hesitated for a long moment, like he had to mentally edit down his speech. "I committed what you Americans would call tax fraud."

I stared at him. That was a way less exciting explanation than I was hoping for, and suddenly, I was having painful flashbacks to my last time in prison. "You guys don't happen to know a John Dowe, do you?"

"John Dowe? Isn't that the guy they just brought into the morgue?" Ryan asked.

Vance slapped a hand on the table. "No, that's Tony. I keep telling them, but they won't believe me. If they pull the dental records, they'll see I'm telling the truth."

I leaned my elbows on the table and pinched my temples. "What are the odds?" I moaned.

"Odds of what?" Vance asked.

I stopped rubbing my head long enough to glare at him. "Huh?"

"You said 'what are the odds.' I can't calculate the odds unless I have all the data points. What probability are you trying to estimate?"

The statement was delivered without even the tiniest hint of sarcasm, and I abruptly realized that Vance and I would not get along well.

I swung my legs over the bench and stood up.

"Hey, you didn't eat!" Ryan protested.

"I'm late for my shift," I lied, and strode towards the door.

I was almost to the hall when the Lord stopped me. *You turn around and head right back to that table, young man.*

"Why should I?" I snapped.

It hit me like a lightning strike. I stumbled against the door frame as my mind briefly left this plane of existence. The images flashed by too rapidly for me to discern all the details, but I saw enough to know that the vision was about Vance and Ryan—and the Lord had big things planned.

God waited until I repossessed my body before speaking again. *Don't ask questions you don't want the answers to.*

"All right then, I won't," I returned, and went to take another step.

He slapped me with it again. I could make out more of the details this time. It had something to do with this factory—and I was right there with them.

I shouted a choice word I probably shouldn't have used in the presence of the Lord. "Really?" I yelled, throwing my hands up to the ceiling. "Is this really what You want?"

Several guards looked my way, but they quickly decided that me shouting like a deranged idiot at empty space wasn't enough of a threat, and their attention drifted.

I realized I'd better make my conversation internal before someone else tried to join it. *I thought we went over this yesterday—I need to get back to Phil.*

Stop using her as an excuse.

I froze as all my arguments shriveled up and died.

He took advantage of my rare state of speechlessness. *I meant what I said. But you can't even obey Me long enough to sit at a table and have lunch with two friendly guys. Why should I trust you to take care of Philadelphia?*

I grimaced as the conviction rolled over me. He was right—Philadelphia *didn't* need me, not in this state. She didn't need another father who was selfish, reckless, and stubborn.

She already had one of those.

The silence in the heavens was patient and forgiving. I closed my eyes, took a deep breath—and gave up.

All right. If there's something You want me to do in this prison, show me.

I just did.

I tugged on my mustache. *Do I really have to bring them along for the ride?*

For an answer, a fragment of the vision flashed through my mind again—and it was definitely Vance and Ryan standing there.

"Will You stop that!" I protested aloud.

I told you not to ask questions you didn't want the answers to.

I groaned. Clearly, I wouldn't make any progress towards my goal until I helped Vance and Ryan achieve theirs. "Fine! I'm going!" I conceded. "But I'm pretty sure this qualifies as blackmail."

He didn't deny it. I spun on my heel, ignoring the amused stares from the guards, and strode back to the table.

Ryan saw me approach and waved wildly, as if I was in danger of walking past them. I marched up and leaned my knuckles on the table. "All right! We can be friends," I announced.

"Yay!" Ryan cheered.

"Who said anything about being friends?" Vance grunted.

I lifted my hand. "On one condition."

"Anything," Ryan swore.

"Not you." I turned to Vance. "There's one thing I need to make perfectly clear, sir."

He arched a bushy eyebrow.

"About 95% of the questions I ask are rhetorical and should *not* be answered. Understood?" I stabbed my finger in his face for emphasis.

His eyebrow relaxed as his face flatlined again. "I make no promises."

15: PHILADELPHIA

I hid in the shadows in the hallway, once again preparing to go out on stage and speak to the congregation. Only this time, it wasn't the Tangs' church. This time, I would be ministering to a congregation in the neighboring city of Tianjin.

I'd attended five churches in as many days. Most of the pastors had been friends of Bowen, but this church had sought me out. They'd sent a messenger to the factory with a gift, begging me to come speak.

Lanzhou had been hesitant; we didn't know these people. But Jael had been delighted and agreed immediately. After all, this meant my plan was working.

I'd presented my idea to Bowen first: Let me go on tour and speak to churches and other unassimilated groups throughout the city. If people trusted me, then letting them see my face was the best way to repair the damage Jayde and Asia had done. I could rally the troops and demonstrate that I was on the ground, fighting alongside them. I would show the world that Asia had not intimidated me—and the more people felt emboldened by my presence, the more our numbers would grow.

Bowen had been enthusiastic about the idea, as I suspected, and Jael took surprisingly little convincing. It was Lanzhou who insisted on being the voice of reason. I was still the most wanted woman in the United, and the more I went out in public, the greater the risk that Asia would find me. His fears weren't unfounded, but I didn't care. After all, I didn't stay in China because it was safe.

He'd been pacified when Jael promised to send security. The black-suited, heavily armed bodyguards seemed to calm Lanzhou, but they had the opposite effect on me. Having security made me feel pretentious, like I was above all these civilians who risked their lives every day to go to church. Even now, my guards stood on either side of the door that led to the meeting room, their expressions masked by dark shades as they frowned in my direction.

I shivered and turned away to face the window, trying to focus my thoughts back on my mission. *This isn't about you—it's about the people behind that door.*

I closed my eyes and tried to picture the faces I'd seen when I'd met with the pastor before service. This congregation was different than the ones I'd spoken to before. This church was comprised entirely of businesspeople—most of whom were highly successful and very influential, according to Bowen. Everyone I'd met so far had been dressed immaculately and carried an air of money. Even their secret meeting place was opulent: They met on the top floor of a glittering high-rise—a floor that didn't exist, based on the buttons in the elevator. The one-way windows in the hall afforded a dizzying view of the city, with the bustling harbor out one side and a glittering Ferris wheel out the other.

Thankfully, Narissa made sure I was dressed for the occasion. She'd sent over a sharp skirt set and black patent shoes with just enough heel to make me look like an adult. As the finishing touch, she'd included the pearl necklace Asia had given me—a classy act of defiance.

I fingered the smooth beads and tried to swallow the feeling of inadequacy I always got right before I took the stage. Normally, if I took a moment to speak in tongues and make room for the Holy Spirit, the feeling faded, but not this time. I never had problems speaking to the churches in the slums; it was easy to give hope to people who had none. But these people were rich;

they didn't worry about the same things. They had different problems, which meant they needed different solutions.

What do they need to hear?

I looked up and caught my reflection in the window. If it weren't for my brown hair and brown eyes, I would have passed as Andromeda Nolan. And that's when I remembered—I *was* one of them. Andromeda was rich. Andromeda had influence. Andromeda had power and family name that could move mountains—but she still needed to hear from God.

The nervousness faded when I realized I had my answer. *What is God saying to me?*

Just then, Bowen came out of the door and gestured at me. I straightened my skirt, found a smile, and followed him into the conference room.

The open hall was crowded with black suits and navy dresses. All hands were in the air as men in ties and women with three-inch heels worshipped with just as much enthusiasm as the factory workers. The moan of prayer in a language I didn't understand filled the room like incense.

I took a deep breath of it and strode up the stairs to the podium. The crowd silenced unbidden as someone introduced me. Walking to the edge of the stage, I held out my hand and gave them exactly what the Lord had given me.

"You're in this position for a reason."

Lanzhou stood beside me and translated into Mandarin, the intensity of his voice matching mine.

"You are not a mistake. Your success is not an accident. Every single thing that brought you to this place was of the Lord. Don't waste it."

I flinched when the words hit the inside of my ribs like a stab of pain. *Please, God, help me not waste this. I know You put me here for a reason. Show me what You want me to do.*

In response, the words came faster. "He gives seed to the sower and talents to those who are faithful—so be faithful! All your money, all your influence, all your political connections—those aren't for you. Those are for the Kingdom of God. The Lord put you here because you have an assignment, and now is the time to do it!"

I paused to let Lanzhou catch up. All eyes were on me as the silence returned. "God invested in you," I whispered, speaking as much to myself as to them. "And like any good businessman, He's expecting a return. Now is the time to give Him what He's due."

Commotion swept across the room as several people dropped to their knees and started praying. I raised my hand and my voice with it. "'Look, I am coming soon! My reward is with Me, and I will give to each person according to what they have done.' So, I ask you—what have you done?"

I needn't have said any more. The Holy Spirit took control as conviction washed over the crowd. Almost everyone responded, breaking out in prayer or weeping. I set the microphone down and sank to my knees, shuddering as the fear of God dropped on my shoulders.

God had chosen me to be Blue Fire. I knew beyond a shadow of a doubt that was true, and I wanted nothing more than to please Him. And I knew this—worshipping in church and encouraging His people—gave Him joy.

Then why did I feel like I was still falling short?

It was three hours later by the time we left the building. Service had gone on for a while, and then the congregation hosted us for dinner. I barely got a bite in between all the handshaking as Lanzhou struggled to translate the constant stream of thanks.

As with the other churches I'd spoken at, everyone seemed to have brought a gift. I'd been informed that it was considered polite in China to refuse a gift once or twice before accepting, which was convenient, because my genuine reaction was to tell people to stop. It seemed wrong to accept gifts from the church, but everyone gave with such joy that I didn't know how to refuse them. So, I let Bowen collect the growing pile of flowers and jewelry and resisted the urge to cry.

I was grateful when Lanzhou finally led me away. We had almost made it to the elevator when I heard someone running after us, shouting in Mandarin. I turned—but not as fast as my guards. They instinctively stepped in front of me as a breathless businessman approached.

He stopped a respectful distance away and bowed. "*Lei niao*," he greeted.

I dipped my head in acknowledgement. It meant "thunderbird" and was one of the few Mandarin phrases I'd managed to pick up, despite having been in the country for nearly a month.

The man smiled and rattled off a question in Mandarin. I looked to Lanzhou for a translation.

"He says he organizes a prayer group that meets tonight," Lanzhou explained. "He's asking if you would give him the honor of attending."

I smiled and opened my mouth to reply, but Bowen spoke first. "She can't tonight. I've already made another appointment."

Lanzhou apologized to the businessman, who nodded graciously and left.

"Where are we going?" I asked, and hoped I didn't sound as exhausted as I felt.

Instead of answering, Bowen held my black duffle out to me. "You'll want to change."

I did as I was told, ditching my heels and switching back to the military jacket and cargo pants Narissa had designed. My guards escorted me down to the parking garage, where Lanzhou and Bowen were waiting. A giant black SUV with the United seal on the side was idling in front of the door.

I froze as an instinctive wave of fear washed over me. Bowen touched my elbow. "It's okay, they're friends, I promise."

I couldn't read the characters on the side of the vehicle, but Lanzhou must have recognized the logo. He glared at Bowen and barked a question in Mandarin.

"It's fine, they know we're coming," Bowen answered in English. He guided me towards the car. "She deserves to see it for herself."

"See what for myself?" I demanded.

Bowen grinned at me. "You don't just have churches supporting you."

Everything about this situation made me uneasy, but I climbed into the backseat of the vehicle when one of my guards opened the door. Two of them slid in beside me as Bowen took shotgun next to the driver. I sat up straight and tried not to fidget as we drove out of town.

Within an hour, the bustling highways and manicured green spaces gave way to the austere concrete ocean of factories and shipping yards. Towers of rusted shipping containers blocked out the setting sun as we passed the docks that were the lifeblood of Tianjin's industry.

Abruptly, the road ended in a concrete wall. The top of the barricade was lined with barbed wire, and the United flag flew from every corner. Sniper towers stood watch over the complex, the tips of their rifles seeming to follow us as we rolled up to the electrified metal gate. I leaned forward and caught a glimpse of a parked tank in the yard—and suddenly, I knew where we were.

A military base.

"Bowen..." I started, panic closing my throat.

"I told you, they're friends. You need to see this." He nodded at the driver, who began to pull forward slowly. The base evidently *did* know we were coming; the guards at the gate took one look at the license plate on our vehicle and let us in. Our driver didn't even roll his window down.

The gate groaned like the yawning jaws of a tiger as it pulled back into the wall. We drove into the yard and circled around to the office at the back of the complex. All across the lawn, troops were training in groups of a hundred. The rhythmic stamping of feet and the shouting of orders created a sinister symphony as we were dropped off at the main building and hustled inside.

Half a dozen ranking officers were waiting to meet us, their black uniforms dripping with medals. Someone gave an announcement in Mandarin, and all six saluted me. *"Lei niao!"* they shouted in practiced unison.

One of the officers stepped forward and bowed. "Blue Fire, this is Jin *Shao jiang*—Major General Jin," Bowen introduced. "His entire regiment has vowed to defect to you on operation day."

My ears rang as his words thundered in the cavity in my chest. "What?" I croaked.

General Jin gestured. "Come and see."

He led us up a floor to a balcony that overlooked the yard. He guided me to the railing, then pulled a whistle from his jacket. The sharp sound split the air, immediately silencing the activity in the yard. All the personnel turned to look up at the balcony, their faces anonymous in the long shadows of the setting sun.

General Jin flashed a signal with his hands, then called to his troop, his voice carrying across the entire yard. The regiment responded in unison. Like one being, every single soldier spun on his heel to face me. They threw salutes, their arms moving in rhythm like cogs on a machine, and shouted a military chant. The only word I understood was *"lei niao,"* but I knew what the chant meant.

This army answered to me.

The yard grew eerily still as all the soldiers lowered their arms and stood at attention. General Jin trilled another command on his whistle. The regiment immediately fell into formation, the clusters of soldiers rearranging themselves into precise lines as if guided by an unseen magnet. A commander at the head of the crowd shouted, and all the soldiers echoed back. On cue, they began to march across the yard, parading in front of us. As each row passed under the balcony, they saluted by moving the tip of their rifles from their left shoulders to their right. The sound of their boots stamping the concrete filled the air like thunder.

I gripped the railing, desperate not to fall over as the world spun. *God, what is going on?*

"Five thousand soldiers report directly to me," General Jin narrated from somewhere in my peripheral. "We are armed with fifty tanks, ten anti-aircraft guns, two intercontinental ballistic missiles..."

His voice blurred as he continued to catalog his artillery. I pinched my eyes shut, my vision flashing black and blue. What was I supposed to do with five thousand armed soldiers and a storehouse of heavy machinery?

"Does Jael know about this?" I managed.

"Of course," Bowen responded. "She's been coordinating the efforts across the country."

"We have spies in a dozen other regiments, sowing propaganda," General Jin added. "Our hope is that several more troops will pledge allegiance to you before operation day."

I felt Bowen step up beside me. "If enough of the army defects, the government won't be able to retaliate."

He was right. If enough of the army fell to our cause, the government wouldn't be able to strike back.

But we would.

I forced my eyes back open. I watched as row after row of upheld rifles passed beneath me, the polished tips gleaming like shark's teeth. "And what will all of these troops do on operation day?" I whispered, afraid of the answer.

General Jin smiled. "Whatever you command, Blue Fire."

16: PHILADELPHIA

Later that night, I sat on my bed and rewatched my newest video.

Thanks to Jael, I now had a team of professionals editing my content. My videos were no longer just me staring at a camera and narrating; they were fast-paced, trendy productions that made it look like we had the world on our side. Clips from my rallies were interspersed with moving graphics, compromising footage of government officials, and anonymous testimonies from civilians who had joined the cause. All of it was overlaid with fiery audio as I screamed into the microphone under the power of the Holy Spirit and urged people to wake up and see what was right in front of them.

This latest video was particularly scathing. It began with me listing the United's ethical atrocities, my voice catching as I recited the gruesome statistics of oppression and genocide. As I narrated, a whirlwind of classified photos flashed across the screen, including several showing the depravity inside the religious containment camps I had once called home. Then my voice changed pitch as the images melded into clips of my acts of rebellion. Suddenly, those same oppressed people were joining me as we broke my old neighbors out of camp and gathered as a praising mob in church, lifting our hands and falling on our faces without fear of the government.

The video culminated in a call to action, carefully scripted by Jael: *"You can end the United. You can save the world."* The last image before the screen went dark was a clip from my visit to the military base. I stood on the balcony, the setting sun flaring behind me, as a hundred armed soldiers saluted. The footage had been carefully cropped so you couldn't pinpoint the location, and the only face in focus was mine. But the message was clear: This was war, and I had an army behind me.

I paused the video. Is that what Operation Blue Fire had become: a call for war? I'd always known that resistance would bring some bloodshed. The United would retaliate, and they would not be kind. But their sins were on their own hands, and I didn't have to play by their rules. I'd never thought of my acts of rebellion as war; I just wanted to be brave enough to say "no."

Did I still believe that? Would the scattered resistance of a hundred thousand civilians be enough to end the system? Or were Bowen and my uncle right—had I been put in this place to do more?

"You're not a civilian anymore, and you can't afford to think like one."

My chest tightened. It didn't hurt, but it was that off-kilter feeling that told me I wasn't seeing the whole picture. It was like I was about to complete a puzzle, but one piece was missing.

I flopped back on the pillows and stared at the carved clouds that circled the top of the bed frame. "Is this what You want, God?" I asked into the soft darkness. "Is this why I'm Blue Fire?"

I closed my eyes and listened, but all I could hear was the rustling of the river and the distant grind of traffic.

I sighed. I knew silence meant "keep asking," but still I wondered, not for the first time, how much easier this would be if God would just *show* me things like He showed Nic.

What would it be like to see visions? God had spoken to me before, but never like that. What would it be like to hear the voice of God all the time, clear as day, like He was a friend sitting across the table? How would it feel to be trusted with snippets of the future like Isaiah and Jeremiah? If someone like Nic could prophesy, was it possible that I could learn to do it, too?

Sadly, I would never get to ask Nic about his experiences. I flinched when the repressed grief hit the back of my throat. *I miss him, God. I need him right now.*

My tablet pinged. I picked it up, expecting a message from Stanyard—but it wasn't. It was a friend request from a username I'd never seen before, and the content of their text made my heart freeze.

HEY, IT'S DATA. CAN WE TALK?

I jerked upright. Why was Data texting me? Surely, it wouldn't have been that hard for him to find out my username, but he and I hadn't talked since I left Boston. And even before that, I'm not sure we'd ever had what would constitute a full conversation. The fact that he wanted to call now could only mean one thing.

I opened the app and considered blocking the message, but I felt that breath in the Spirit that told me everything was going to be okay. After muttering a prayer, I accepted his friend request. I hit dial before I could second guess myself, but I disabled my video.

He had no such reservations. He answered immediately, and his video connected to reveal him sitting in a cluttered office. He looked a lot like Stanyard, with his headphones hanging around his neck and the backlit glare of his screens highlighting his face in blue. The only difference was that Data had at least three times the number of monitors; the whole side wall of his office was paneled with them, making the room look like the bridge on a spaceship.

"Hey," he initiated, his eyes roaming the screen as if expecting me to appear out of a corner. "Thanks for answering."

I decided I didn't have the patience for the preamble. "What do you want?"

"Look, I think we both know what this is about."

"Do we?" I challenged, and hoped he could read the threat in my tone of voice.

"Phil," he sighed, sounding almost bored, "I have access to every single byte of information on the base's server. As soon as Stanyard started running searches for my name, I found out about it."

I swallowed a wave of trepidation and waited.

He leaned forward. "Is there something you want to ask me?"

I gritted my teeth. "Did you try to kill Nic?"

"No," he answered, voice calm and unashamed. "I bought the code for the DNA off the black market. I had no idea it was programmed for more than one person."

I chewed on my lip. In some weird way, I almost wished he had said yes. At least then, I would have reason to believe him.

He seemed to read the meaning behind my silence. "If you want me to prove it, I will. I'll give Stanyard access to anything he wants. This is the laptop I used to code your chip." He held the device up. "I'll give it to him tomorrow and he can scan the whole thing. He'll find the change log for the code, all the text messages I had with Jayde, and the email I got from my source. He can even search my phone if he wants to cross-reference it."

I sighed. The fact that Data was going out of his way to prove his innocence reinforced what I already suspected: It wasn't him. But this was all still hearsay, and even I was smart enough to realize that it was too soon to trust him. If Data really wanted to cover his tracks, he would edit the device before he gave it to Stanyard. The only way to definitively prove that he didn't do it would be to find out who did.

And we weren't any closer to answering that question.

"What do you want me to say?" I groaned finally.

"Nothing. I don't expect you to trust me." He put his hands up dismissively.

"Then why did you call?"

"Because there's something else you should know." He grunted and glanced away, as if he were afraid to admit what was coming next. "I figured out how they got the code for Nic's DNA."

I gripped the bedspread. "How?"

He looked back at the camera. "They used your credentials."

My heart stopped, then restarted in a panic like someone was holding a gun to my chest. "But I didn't—"

"I know *you* didn't do it," he snorted, as if that was the most ludicrous idea he'd ever heard. "Unless you're really good at setting up a proxy chain."

I wagged my head, not that he could see it. I didn't even know what a proxy chain was.

"You suggested to Stanyard that they might have gotten the DNA off the door lock software from the base on Mars, and you were right." Data leaned forward and typed on a keyboard as he explained. "I used Jayde's old login to access the software before Ephesus wiped the server, and according to the logs, someone used your credentials to access the database and download the code. You had the clearance."

I remembered what Ephesus had said about Nic granting me Level 2 security clearance. Not only had I used my privileges to destroy the base, but apparently, I'd also given someone the keys to kill Nic.

This really *was* all my fault.

I gripped my stomach and tried not to be sick. "But how did they get my credentials?"

Data shrugged. "Depends on how they accessed the system. They could have hacked into a device registered to Andromeda and used it as a proxy. Or if they were on Mars, they might have just used a voice clip or DNA sample to access a terminal. Realistically, anyone with full security access on Jayde's team could have done it, if they were smart enough."

Including you, I thought but didn't bother to say. I knew Data wouldn't spell his plan out to me if he was guilty.

"I can send you the screenshots," he offered.

"Please," I said, even though I believed him.

He clicked his mouse several times, and my tablet pinged. "I'm trying to trace the IP, but like I said, either our criminal is working from Jupiter, or they set up a wickedly good proxy chain." He leaned back in his chair. "I'll keep digging. My best guess is that our killer downloaded the DNA and bribed my source in the black market to add it to his code, but I haven't been able to prove it. I'll let you know if I find anything concrete."

"Thanks," I mumbled. I had no reason to be optimistic.

Data let me nurse the silence for a moment, then dragged his chair closer to the desk. "Look, there's another reason I called."

"What?" I sighed, exhausted.

"It's about your videos. I think it's time to go wide."

I frowned at the screen. "Go wide?"

He spun his chair to face one of the monitors on the side wall. "I've been working for the last month to expand our broadcasting capabilities. If we're going to win this thing, your videos need to be seen by more people."

He dragged his mouse to expand a window, filling the screen with a ream of code. He pointed at it like he expected the technical gibberish to mean something to me. "Thanks to an in at the local news station, I've coded a backdoor into the program the United uses for compulsory announcements. With a couple of clicks, I can use that program to push your videos onto every single registered device on the planet—and boost the live feed on all the social networks."

The words sounded so fantastical that I was sure I hadn't heard right. "I'm sorry, what?"

"You've seen a compulsory announcement, right?"

It was an inane question; that was the whole nature of compulsory announcements. They were always prefaced with a hideous beep like a tornado siren, and then the video would autoplay on every registered device like a virus. The government used them for "important" announcements, like new regulations and public executions.

"There's a fancy program they use to populate those videos. Every registered device has it installed. Now that I'm in the system, all I have to do is plug one of your videos into the program, and suddenly Blue Fire is mandatory viewing."

I sucked in my breath so hard my ribs hurt. Jael had hijacked a few obscure channels in Beijing, but that was nothing compared to what Data was promising. If he was telling the truth, we could bypass the algorithm and force the entire world to watch. We could use the United's own technology against them and bring the entire system crashing down in minutes.

All without firing a single shot.

"We need to test it," Data stressed, his voice cautious. Flickering code reflected in his eyes as he typed a command on his keyboard. "As soon as we broadcast something, they'll be working around the clock to patch my backdoor. I want to run a couple of tests in localized areas—say, Boston—so I can see how they react and create some workarounds for their fixes. It's going to take a couple of weeks, and I'll need Jael's help."

He turned back to the camera. "Again, I'm not asking you to trust me," he said, as if anticipating my objections. "Just give my contact information to Jael. I will give her all my access codes and let her do it herself if she wants. And if she doesn't take it— well, at least I tried."

"Why are you doing this?" I blurted. If Data was being honest, then he was willing to sacrifice his entire livelihood for the cause. He was willing to hand me the keys to his digital empire free of charge—and I didn't even know his real name.

He smiled, his eyes glinting in the glare from his screens. "I'm in this for you, Blue Fire. I know you can do this. So, let me help you win this war."

17: NIC

The third week of my incarceration was mind-numbingly uneventful.

Ryan, who was apparently something of a supervisor, convinced the warden to transfer me to his shift by promising he would keep an eye on me. This he did religiously. He rearranged the schedule so I was always working within three yards of him, and he insisted we take every break together. He even pulled some strings and got my bunk assignment moved to the same cell as him and Vance, much to my dismay.

He needn't have bothered. I was under strict orders from the Lord not to cause trouble for either of them. So, I shut up and did as I was told—much to the surprise of management. Warden Ivanova was so suspicious of my sudden compliance that she sent guards to check on me for the first few days, just to make sure I hadn't escaped.

I told her that if the Lord ever gave me permission to run again, she'd be the first to know.

Eventually, everyone got over the spectacle, and Vance, Ryan, and I settled into a boring rhythm. And I mean *boring* literally; taking laps around Rott had been more intellectually stimulating than this. My job on the assembly line was so pedestrian that a ten-year-old could have done it. In fact, had they rearranged the line a little bit, I could have done my job, Vance's, *and* Ryan's all at the same time—and met a higher quota.

I wasn't about to volunteer myself for more work, but a reformation would have saved them a lot of money. I remembered what Warden Ivanova had said about production being down, and I wasn't surprised the higher ups had docked her pay. I would have fired her, personally. It was a crime how poorly this factory was being run. The assembly line was gloriously inefficient, the guards' and workers' schedules were a hot mess, and the resource waste was scandalous. The only part of the operation Warden Ivanova had down to a science was the discipline.

The Lord consistently pointed out all the ways the factory could be improved, as if me and my three doctorates couldn't clearly see it for ourselves. In fact, that was all He wanted to talk about. I would have preferred to talk about His vision for Vance and Ryan; the sooner I could figure out His end game, the sooner I could get this show on the road and earn my way out of here. But He insisted on dissecting the entire operation until I could have written a master thesis on the subject.

I wasn't sure why I needed this information. I couldn't do anything about it; my job was simply to show up and let Ryan boss me around. And even if I could make some changes, I wouldn't want to. Why would I want to improve my own prison? If these communists wanted to bankrupt themselves with a failed business venture, let them.

This went on for several days, with the Lord pointing out inefficiencies and me pretending not to care. In an effort to avoid conversation with anybody, I practiced memorizing the digits of pi. At least *that* was information I would probably use later.

It had been a particularly monotonous shift, and I had just recited to the 3,587th digit when the Lord rudely interrupted.

You know you can fix this, right? You could save this factory.

I groaned. "Are You still on about that?"

"Ay yi, talking to yourself again, Q?" Ryan peeked out from behind the machine. "Tell Him I said hi!"

I looked up at the ceiling. "Ryan says hi."

"Vance says hi too!"

Vance leaned out from around the other side of the machine. "I said no such thing."

"I'm just putting in a good word for you, buddy."

I squatted down and pretended to fiddle with a control panel so I wouldn't have to look at either of them. "Yes, I'm fully aware I have the *ability* to reform this entire operation," I hissed, keeping my voice down. "What I fail to recognize is why I should care."

I didn't ask you to care. I asked you to obey.

I growled and hurled my wrench on the floor with a terrific clang.

"Oy, sounds like Q lost the argument again," Ryan whispered, as if I couldn't hear him.

"I don't believe it's theologically possible to win an argument with the Lord," Vance whispered back.

"What do you call that deal where Abraham was like, 'What if I find one righteous dude?'"

"First of all, that wasn't an argument. Second of all, that passage illustrates a very important theological point about intercession—"

"Enough!" I shouted, loud enough for them *and* the entire floor to hear me. "I can't take it anymore." I turned and stomped off.

"Wait! Don't do it, Q!" Ryan scampered after me. "Don't jump!"

"I'm not going to jump." I reached the elevator and punched the button. "I'm going to fix their efficiency output."

He skidded to a stop. "Their what now?"

I didn't bother to answer him. I stepped onto the elevator and called Level 57. If Warden Ivanova was on schedule today, she should be supervising the unloading of supplies on Dock 12.

She was running a few minutes behind, but I caught her as she strode around the corner to the docking bay, her usual entourage of guards in tow.

She paused to give me a sniveling look down her nose. "What are you doing here?"

"Talking to you. You're late—did your Monday conference call go over?"

"How did you—never mind." She shook her head and brushed past me. "I thought we'd mutually decided not to talk to each other again, Q. And you were doing so well. Get him back to his station."

The latter comment was directed at the guards, but I sidestepped them and ran after her. "I know, but if I don't get this off my chest, I won't be able to live with myself."

Or, more accurately, I won't be able to live with the Holy Spirit.

She halted. "Please tell me you're not about to propose."

"You're a… fascinating woman, but no. Remember how you said production was down, and they'd docked your pay?"

"Thanks for announcing that in front of literally everybody." She glared at her guards, who conveniently looked elsewhere like they hadn't heard.

"Well, I'm here to tell you I can fix it."

The elevator opened, and Vance and Ryan ran towards us.

Warden Ivanova snorted. "Sounds like a scam."

"I'm serious. I've been analyzing this factory for three weeks now, and I've identified twenty-one ways you can increase production today. None of them will cost you anything except the time it takes to implement them—and we might need to do some maintenance in Shaft 5 to fix the load distribution issue."

My coworkers reached us. "Sorry, ma'am," Ryan panted, extremely out of breath. "We tried to stop him, but he's got really long legs."

The warden put up a hand to silence him. "And why should I believe you?" she challenged, eyes on me.

I hesitated. *"Because the Lord spoke to me"* would have been the correct answer, but probably not the one she wanted to hear.

Vance spared me the misery. "He's right, ma'am," he said, stepping up. "This factory is operating at roughly 57% efficiency.

You're easily losing twenty grand in revenue a month, and that's a conservative estimate. I've run the calculations myself."

I gawked at him. "And you didn't say anything before now? You've been here, what, a decade? If I find out the Lord sent me here just because you were too lazy to say something, I *will* kick you."

He shrugged. "I don't publish my findings until they've been reviewed by expert peers."

One of the guards jabbed his thumb at me. "What about him? He's got three PhDs."

Vance squinted, as if weighing my competency. "Is one of them in biomechanical engineering?"

"Um, lemme look." The guard pulled out his device and started scrolling through it.

Before I could object to details of my personnel file being shared without my consent, Warden Ivanova mercifully intervened. "Enough! Look, since you're the 'doctor' here, I'm going to ask you." She locked eyes with me. "Is this true?"

I straightened. "Yes. If you give me a computer, I can have a full report and a model simulation on your desk by Friday."

She arched an eyebrow. "And what do I get out of it?"

"Besides increased profits and a raise?" I held her gaze. "If you don't believe me, then let's do a bet. If you want to test my theories for a month, I'll put my life up as collateral. Implement my model, and if your productivity hasn't increased by at least 20% in thirty days, you can take it out on me."

The words slipped out before I could properly ingest them. That's when I registered—far too late to back out—that it wasn't me speaking.

Now look what You've gotten us into!

I've got your back, He coolly replied.

"Aww man," Ryan whined, "I was just getting used to having more than one friend."

Warden Ivanova's face cracked in a wicked grin. "I love a good wager. Fine, you've got yourself a deal, Q. One month, and you don't touch anything until you've run the plans by me, understood?"

I offered her my hand. "Done."

She shook it violently. "I can't *wait* to see how this goes."

18: PHILADELPHIA

Early on a Tuesday morning, I sat in the recording studio and prepared to hijack one of China's most popular networks.

It was going to be our first live test. Jael, Data, and their team of moles in the media had been working around the clock to bulletproof our control over the system. We started by running several innocuous tests; Data commandeered the signal during off-peak hours and broadcasted a graphic that said "technical difficulties." The hope was that if anyone caught it, they would assume it was a system error instead of a hacker.

The ruse worked. Data watched to see how quickly the network responded and what steps they took to restore service, then adapted his program to compensate. Stanyard pulled overtime helping him rewrite the code; even Ephesus pitched in, traveling to a nearby base so he could come online and assist the team for a few days. After a week of testing, Data was able to take control of a channel and keep broadcasting the graphic for over fifteen minutes before the network finally took themselves offline.

After that, we started sinking our teeth into more popular networks. At first, we would interrupt the broadcast only for a second, flashing up the thunderbird symbol and then immediately restoring the regular programming. Sometimes, it was so fast that the anchormen didn't even notice they'd been hijacked, but we knew the people were seeing it.

Then we started streaming video clips. They were short at first; most of them were just my face in a nearly dark room as I hauntedly repeated, *"Can anyone hear me? It's Blue Fire. I need your help,"* over and over.

That got the government's attention. They reacted swiftly; my next broadcast was shut down in seconds. Data adapted his code, and it took the government three minutes to stop my next stream. Then five, then ten.

We started broadcasting whole videos then. All my old streams were republished, aired on a random network at a random time so that the government wouldn't know where to look. We let the videos loop over and over, filling the screens of millions of devices until the censors finally found us and took the networks offline.

We knew we were making progress when gossip about the hijackings began to escape the algorithm and circulate on social media. Civilians who had never heard of "Operation Blue Fire" were now talking about me as I repeatedly usurped their favorite programming. Meanwhile, studio executives began to complain about the government's lack of response, which was almost as damaging to United morale as my videos themselves. The internet was starting to do my job for me—and that's when we knew it was time to go live.

I stared at my reflection in the curved camera lens and tried to appreciate the magnitude of what was about to happen. In less than two minutes, I would be commandeering one of mainland China's most-watched morning talk shows. Over a hundred and fifty million people were about to get snapped out of their complacency as their daily routine was disrupted by my desperate call for help.

This would be our biggest broadcast yet. Jael had warned me that I would likely get shut down quickly, but Data was confident he could have us back up and running within twenty-four hours. If this worked—if we were able to keep me live on China's largest network for even a few minutes—then that was a sign we were almost ready to go wide. Once Data fully perfected his code, we would pull the trigger, and my broadcast would simultaneously hijack every registered device between here and Mars. Every connected citizen in the United would see me.

After that, even the government wouldn't be able to stop Operation Blue Fire.

I looked up to see Jael moving behind the plexiglass window of the control booth. The giant digital clock behind her counted down, the seconds seeming to fly by faster than time itself.

Twenty-nine, twenty-eight…

"Remember," Jael coached over the speaker, "you may only have a minute. So, open strong and talk fast."

Fifteen, sixteen…

I inhaled through my nose and nodded.

Ten, nine…

I pinched my eyes shut and squeezed out a final prayer. *Holy Spirit, speak through me.*

Three… two… one.

I opened my eyes and stared straight at the camera.

"My name is Philadelphia Smyrna, and I'm here to tell you that the United's days are numbered."

*

I stumbled out of the recording studio in a drunk daze. The broadcast had been an exhilarating success. Data had managed to keep my stream up for a heroic eight minutes and fifty two seconds—long enough that I ran out of prepared remarks and had to go off-script. For nearly nine minutes, I held the captive attention of the nation as I told the world about Operation Blue Fire. I spelled out the government's doom as I told China exactly what the revolution—civilian and military alike—would do on operation day.

At precisely 9am on Thursday, September 17th—a date that had been significant for freedom and peace more than once—the revolution would start. Bureaucrats would quit their government jobs. Clerks would burn paperwork and delete files. Teachers would tell their students the truth about why the United was created. Policemen and containment camp guards would lay down their weapons. Civilians everywhere would stand up and say no.

At precisely 9am on Thursday, September 17th, 2076, the world would end, and the new one would begin.

John and Dowe met me outside the recording studio with loud cheers and crushing hugs. Bowen was next in line; he pumped my hand in both of his and grinned. "Now *that's* a revolution."

I shakily returned the smile, bumping into the door frame as I struggled to regain control of my nerves.

Lanzhou touched my shoulder. "You okay?" he said gently.

I wasn't; I hadn't been for a week. I couldn't keep up with all this. The revolution had ignited the world like a forest fire; it was growing so fast and so hot that I couldn't even wrap my mind around what it—what Blue Fire—had become. Even now, the world was spinning so hard that I didn't feel like I possessed my body anymore. But it was a small price to pay for victory.

"Yeah, just dizzy," I fudged.

He frowned. "Come sit down."

He guided me towards the conference room, where Jael and several others were waiting. The network I'd just hijacked was playing on the projector. Service had been restored, but instead of the scheduled talk show, they were running an emergency broadcast. I watched as an ugly picture of me flashed up on the screen, superimposed with the demeaning words "WANTED." A pre-recorded clip of Asia looped in the corner as she prattled about the reward the government was offering in exchange for information about my whereabouts.

I cackled at the irony as I sank into a chair. Clearly, I'd struck a nerve. Blue Fire was turning the tide of war—and Asia knew it.

"Check," I muttered to the screen.

Jael's heels clacked on the floor as she approached me. "Excellent work. Your engagement has increased tenfold.

Activity around your name is surging, especially in demographics we haven't reached before."

She held out her tablet. A bouncing pictograph filled the screen as the algorithm struggled to catalog my popularity.

"A hundred million gossiping housewives will take it from here," Bowen snarked. He winked at me in a way that suggested he had experience with such things.

I started to laugh but realized I didn't have the energy to finish. Lanzhou set a glass of water on the table next to me, and I gratefully took it.

"Hey, I know it's been a big day." Bowen sat down next to me and softened his voice. "But do you feel up to making a visit?"

I glanced at him out of the corner of my eye and contemplated refusing.

Lanzhou did it for me. "Are you sure that's wise? 'A hundred million housewives' just saw her face—the entire country is going to be on high alert. I don't think she should be seen in public at all right now."

He had a point, and that gave even Bowen a slight pause. "We're not bringing cameras to this visit. And... it's a request from a friend."

He reached across the table and grabbed a large white shirt box. He slid it towards me. A note was taped to the top:

THERE'S SOME OLD FRIENDS OF MINE I WOULD LIKE YOU TO VISIT. CALL IT A FAVOR FOR ME—IT WOULD MEAN A LOT. –N

P.S. WEAR THIS

I pulled the note off and handed it to Jael, then lifted the lid of the box. Inside, on a bed of white tissue paper, was my old outfit.

Well, the clothes were new; I could tell the fabric had been freshly minted on Narissa's fabricator. But the garments were modeled exactly after the industrial outfit I used to wear when I lived in the containment camp: a gray jacket and leggings layered with a linen skirt. She'd updated the design a little bit; the fit was more flattering, and the skirt fabric was light and flowy. But the resemblance was unmistakable.

I fingered the tight stitching on the hem. Philadelphia Smyrna was truly back from the dead.

"Of course, I'll go," I murmured. "Anything for Narissa."

"I knew you'd say that. We'll leave in an hour." Bowen grinned and started to rise.

I moved to follow, but Lanzhou gripped the back of my chair and stopped me. "Are you sure about this?" The question was directed at Jael.

She set the note in my lap. "No cameras, and I absolutely do not want her seen from the street. You go in a back way and leave by a different one, and they better keep the shades drawn. Understood?" She arched an eyebrow at Bowen.

He nodded. "I'll make the arrangements."

19: PHILADELPHIA

Narissa's friends lived in an apartment across town. The residential subdistrict was a few miles from downtown and had been developed rapidly to contain the overflow of people from the suffocating inner city. The streets were less crowded and the buildings less imposing; most of the apartment complexes were only a modest fifteen stories tall. It was the perfect place for some rebels to hide in plain sight.

Our driver took us around to the back of the apartment building at the end of the block. We were riding in an unmarked delivery van with forged license plates; the windowless load area afforded some privacy, and the vehicle was unassuming enough. Jael had sent six security guards with me, which seemed like an excess, but I knew better than to argue. They'd dressed down for the occasion, switching their black suits for generic work uniforms and leaving the sunglasses behind. Personally, I preferred the new look.

The apartment's loading dock was open to receive us. A laundry delivery truck idled in the alley, blocking the way. My driver honked twice before the other driver finally looked up from his device. With an impatient glare, he begrudgingly pulled forward so we could back up to the dock.

Bowen jumped out and opened the hatch. The laundry ladies pushed their carts out of my way as the disguised guards hustled me up the service elevator to the third floor.

As soon as the elevator door opened, I realized this wasn't a typical apartment. The sterile scent of bleach fought to overpower the stench of illness and death. It smelled like a hospital, and it sounded like one, too. I heard the beeping of monitors, the murmuring of hushed voices, and the squeak of wheelchair wheels on linoleum. Carts of medical equipment crowded the hall, along with an ominously empty stretcher.

"What is this place?" I dared to ask.

Bowen led the way down the hall. "Think of it as a group home. These are all people who have been rejected from the healthcare system—or rescued from it, depending on who you ask."

I followed him hesitantly, the guards trailing on my heels. The first few doors we passed were shut, but the fourth was cracked open. I heard the blare of a TV from inside.

Bowen rapped on the doorframe with his knuckles and shouted something in Mandarin. He was answered enthusiastically. The door banged open, and a man with no legs appeared.

I jerked back involuntarily. From the waist up, he looked perfectly normal, but his legs were gone. It didn't even look like they'd been amputated; it looked like he'd never had them in the first place.

I realized too late that I was staring. He chuckled disarmingly. "I have that effect on women."

I flushed and offered my hand. "Blue Fire—I mean, Philadelphia."

He grabbed the door frame and used his arms to swing himself out into the hall. "Oh, I know who you are—we all saw your stint on the news." He gestured with his shoulder at his TV while he pumped my hand. "Call me Huan."

I smiled. "Pleased to meet you."

"Now, I know what you're going to ask." He rocked back and put both hands up. "First question I usually get: It's called *amelia*, and it's a rare birth disorder. Second question I usually get: Yes, I'm single." He winked.

Bowen swatted him on the shoulder. "This is why I can't take you anywhere."

"No, the reason you can't take me anywhere is because the government wants to kill me." Huan rolled his eyes. "But Blue Fire would know all about that, wouldn't she?"

I frowned and looked to Bowen for an explanation.

He squeezed Huan's shoulder. "Everyone in this building is on the government's 'do not resuscitate' list. Some, like Huan here, were born with disabilities or deformities."

Huan reached up and patted Bowen's hand. "I'm lucky—I was born in a small village under a midwife, so my parents were able to hide me. For a while, at least."

I thought about Narissa's blind eyes—a deformity that had been corrected by robotic implants—and abruptly realized how she knew these people.

I felt a weight drop to my stomach as the Holy Spirit pressed on my ribs. "I'm sorry," I managed.

Huan shook his head. "Don't be. I have it good here. I'm working an online job under false credentials, and the apartment manager lies about who she's renting to. But if you succeed..." He looked up and met my eyes. "Maybe I can put my name on the mailbox without worrying they're going to take me away."

Narissa's haunting words came floating back to me.

"The government doesn't like imperfect people any more than it likes religious brats."

Bowen gave Huan's shoulder one last squeeze and bid him goodbye in Mandarin, then turned and continued down the hall. "This whole apartment is a sham. All the residents here have been condemned to die for one reason or another. Some have conditions the government deems untreatable."

My eyes scanned the disorganized racks of second-hand medical equipment as I followed him around the corner.

"Others were abandoned as children because they came from parents who weren't supposed to have kids—or from minorities the government thinks we have a 'surplus' of."

He paused and pointed towards an open door. I glanced inside and saw the room was crammed with mismatched cribs. A frazzled nurse bustled about, tending to at least half a dozen squalling babies.

Bowen stepped up behind her and spoke softly. She whipped around, almost smacking him in the face, then relaxed when she saw who it was. Bowen pointed at one of the cribs. The nurse nodded, picked up a child—and walked out into the hall and handed it to me.

I almost dropped it—her, judging by the color of her onesie. I couldn't remember the last time I'd held a baby. I hadn't grown up around children; I was the youngest in my family, and most of the people in camp had stopped having kids.

Suddenly, I wondered if that choice hadn't been voluntary.

Bowen reached up and brushed the baby's dark peach-fuzz hair. "Most children like her aren't even making it out of the womb."

I tightened my grip around the child, causing her to fuss and stir.

"This is what true evil looks like, Phil." Sudden tears clogged Bowen's voice. "I know we've got problems with taxes and fraud and religious oppression—but *this*, murdering innocent children, is what grieves the Savior's heart."

I choked on my next breath. He was right, and America was no better. We'd been killing our own for a century.

Maybe that was why we were in this mess in the first place.

I shoved the baby back at the nurse. "Please, I can't."

She nodded and took the child. Bowen kept walking. "This is why I joined the operation. Yes, I think the government is evil, and yes, I think the world needs to change. But that's not what bothers me. That's not what gets me down on my knees, night after night, begging God to have mercy on my nation. It's these people."

He stopped in the middle of the hall and spread his hands. "When Jesus came to earth, He fought for the diseased, the widows, the Samaritans. He loved the people society rejected. If I don't fight for their right to exist, how can I claim to love the world like He did?"

The room blurred out of focus as my eyes stung with tears. "Bowen, I—"

A heavy *thump* against the wall interrupted me.

I jumped and looked for the source. It was coming from the room a few doors down. I heard it again, and again—a dull beating on the wall, repeated but erratic.

I swallowed. "What's that?"

Bowen smiled sadly. "That's Sienna. Come meet her."

He walked over to the door and opened it softly. I stepped up next to him and looked over his shoulder.

The room was practically bare, completely stripped of breakables and hard edges, and I immediately saw why. In the far corner, a girl only a year or two younger than myself was beating her head into the wall. She had a foam helmet strapped under her chin, but that didn't stop her from incessantly trying to injure herself. The plaster was dented throughout the room, and several holes had been hastily patched with plywood. The window was braced with a board to keep her from banging into the glass.

"Severe autism," Bowen answered my unspoken question.

"But why is she doing that?" I managed, even though I was afraid of the answer.

Bowen rubbed his chin. "Think of it like being chronically overstimulated. There are a lot of things in this world—sounds, bright lights—that her body simply can't process. What's normal to us might be excruciating for her, and repetitive pain is the only way she can distract herself."

I remembered all the times I had slammed my fist into concrete floors, desperate to feel anything but confusion and fear, and thought I might understand, in a sad and incomplete way.

"She'll require lifelong care, which isn't something the government is eager to fund. I'm told they smuggled her out of a hospital where she was going to be euthanized," Bowen explained softly.

I braced myself against the doorframe as the world washed out.

"Come on, there's more I'd like you to meet." Bowen touched my elbow and tried to pull me away.

I couldn't move. I was rooted to the floor as despair drained the blood from my face like water. Blue Fire couldn't help these people. Sure, I could fight for a society that wouldn't kill them, but that wouldn't *save* them. There was no amount of money or power or prestige that could save people like Sienna. I could reform the world, birth a brand-new government, and bring freedom for all—and Sienna would still be stuck in a corner somewhere, banging her head into a wall as the disease of this fallen world stripped her of the woman she was created to be.

A revolution couldn't save her.

I couldn't save her.

"Phil?" Bowen's voice tried to reach me through the waves of fear. "Are you all right?"

Before I could answer him, a gunshot ripped the air.

We all whipped around. Several more shots followed. I heard glass shattering and a door banging, and a muffled scream echoed from a few floors down.

"*Jingcha!* Police!" someone shouted.

My guards drew their weapons. Bowen ran to the nearest window and threw the curtain back. I saw red-and-blue lights flashing off the windows of the building across the street and knew what was happening before he said it.

"They've got the building surrounded! They know you're here."

But how? The question didn't even make it out of my lips. We'd barely been here fifteen minutes, and I'd only talked to three people. Who would have called the police?

Then I remembered Huan's blaring TV and his comment that "everybody" had seen the news. I thought about the whispering laundry workers in the alley—and suddenly, I knew who had turned me in.

Bowen rushed back to me. "We need to get you to the truck, now."

One of my guards stuck out his arm to stop him. "They'll have thought of that. We need another way out of this building."

"There is no other way out!" Bowen shouted. "What, you think we can just walk out the front door?"

Several doors banged open as the apartment's residents poured into the hall. Children cried and nurses shouted for help, and several people called my name. I tried to tune them out as my heart jammed itself up my throat.

Oh God, I can't protect all these people! What have I done?

Bowen continued to bicker with my guards. "We can have another vehicle here in five," one of them insisted, voice calm.

Another gunshot echoed from below. "She won't live that long if we don't get her out of this building!" Bowen screamed.

I pinched my eyes shut and tried to think around the noise. *Holy Spirt, Holy Spirit!* I shrieked over and over, too panicked to get a full prayer out.

Sienna, agitated by the commotion, roared and threw her weight into the wall. I turned to look at her—and saw her boarded-up window.

The idea rammed into me like a brick. "The fire escape!"

It took my guards only a second to catch up. The leader pointed and started barking orders. "You two, with her. Get her to the alley and head to the end of the block—the car will meet you there. If anyone comes into the alley, you shoot first."

Oh Lord, I moaned.

"The rest of you, with me. We're going to stall them in the lobby." The leader flipped the setting on his gun, but I couldn't see what he changed it to. I prayed it was set on stun.

Bowen gripped my arm. "Come on!"

I held back. "Wait!" I grabbed the elbow of the leader. "Please, what about the rest of these people? We have to help them!"

He hesitated for a fraction of a second, his stonewalled eyes scanning me. Then he jerked his head at one of his comrades.

"You, evacuate these people out the fire escape—but keep Blue Fire's path clear! The rest of you, with me!"

He pounded towards the elevator, two of his men falling into line behind him. The third turned and shouted at the confused residents, shepherding them down the hall in the opposite direction.

Bowen hauled me into the room. "Let's go!"

I stumbled after him. The two remaining guards followed, slamming and locking the door behind us. Sienna continued to moan, almost as if she was unaware of our presence.

The guards grabbed the board across the window. With a coordinated yank, the nails ripped from the soft plaster. They threw the board aside, opened the window, and punched the screen out.

One guard climbed out onto the balcony first. He scanned the street below with his gun, then gestured at us. Bowen climbed out after him. He turned and held his hand out to me. "Phil, now!"

The gunshots were getting closer. I heard a scream and the distinct sound of a body hitting the floor and realized the government was taking no prisoners.

"Sienna!" I ran to her and grabbed her arm with both hands. She resisted me, but I begged the Holy Spirit to make me stronger as I dragged her towards the window.

The guard took over. He scooped Sienna up and handed her out the window to his partner. Then he turned and gave me a boost. I hiked up my skirt and slid over the sill, where Bowen caught me.

The wailing of sirens filled the alley, but no one was in sight. The guard tossed Sienna over his shoulder and led the way down the rickety metal stairs. I followed, Bowen and the other guard a step behind me.

We had just reached the ground floor when someone shouted after us. I saw the shadow of a figure entering the alley at the far end. The guard behind me did what he was told: He shot first. I quickly turned away.

Jesus, please! I begged, even though I had no idea what I was asking for.

Commotion filled the alley as the other residents climbed out their windows onto the fire escape. There was no time to look back as the guards hustled us around the corner and down to the end of the block. It seemed like an eternity before we reached the main street. It was like we were running in slow motion, while all around there were screams and gunshots as my guards sacrificed more lives to keep me safe.

Lord, have mercy!

We raced around the last building onto the main road—right into a barricade. Two cop cars blocked the street. I stumbled as the blaring lights blinded me while an officer shouted at us to *"Drop your weapons!"*

The guard in front didn't even hesitate. He shot the nearest officer square in the chest.

Bowen yanked me back around the building as the other officers opened fire. There were six more shots and two screams. A car window shattered. My second guard shielded Sienna with his body as glass rained across the sidewalk.

Finally, the gunshots stopped. Tires squealed and metal crunched. An SUV screeched up to the curb, rear-ending one of the police cars. "Come on!" the first guard yelled at us. He clutched his bleeding shoulder.

I couldn't bring myself to look at the carnage on the street as Bowen hauled me to the car. One guard all but threw Sienna into the backseat, then hoisted me up next to her. He and Bowen crammed in beside us, while the other guard took shotgun and shouted directions to the driver. We peeled away from the curb and raced through a red light, narrowly avoiding a collision.

I struggled to maintain a sense of direction as our driver whipped through side streets. For a horrific moment, I was afraid the motion would never stop, like we were caught in a whirlpool with no way to escape.

But then, finally, our driver slowed, and the world stopped rocking, and the car grew eerily silent. We'd escaped.

I collapsed against the seat, all the adrenaline making my limbs shake as it cycled around in my body with nowhere to go. *What just happened?*

"It's okay, it's okay," Bowen repeated, more to himself than to me. He muttered in tongues. "This is why you have security."

I have security so they can kill people before they kill me. I pinched my eyes shut and willed myself not to be sick. Was this who Blue Fire had become?

Sienna moaned and rammed her head against the window. I pulled her away from the door and wrapped my arms around her. Ignoring her fists pounding into my skin, I closed my eyes and tried to find my center of gravity as my thoughts continued to spiral out of control.

It's not supposed to be this way.

20: PHILADELPHIA

A few hours later, I huddled in a chair at the conference table and trembled while the adults yet again had a heated conversation without me.

We'd made it safely back to the factory, only to find it in an uproar. The United had wasted no time in doctoring and airing the video of the raid. Gruesome footage of bloodied glass and sobbing children was interspersed with sinister shots of medical equipment and dirty linens, making the home look like the set of a horror movie. The anchormen called it inhumane and concocted a story about how the underground was imprisoning sick people and denying them medical care.

But even more damaging was the clip of one of my guards shooting a police officer. The soldier assured me that his weapon had been set on stun, but the United omitted that fact from their reporting. Again and again, they replayed the shot of the officer collapsing, his bodycam glitching as he hit the concrete with a groan. Meanwhile, I ran down the alley in the opposite direction without a single glance back.

That five-second clip was all it took to turn Blue Fire into a violent murderer. Social media exploded with vicious speculation about the real nature of the operation, and the algorithm let it through. Suddenly, the hundred and fifty million people who saw my stream this morning thought I was a dangerous terrorist.

And, in a way, they were right.

My loyal followers immediately responded with the truth, broadcasting their support for me and condemning the government's violent raid. But the damage had been done. It would take weeks of PR to restore the confidence of the Chinese people, let alone the rest of the world.

But that wasn't what worried me. What worried me was all the people I'd just killed. Three of my guards didn't make it back. Several police officers were down. Jael didn't know how many of the home's residents had escaped, but I doubted the numbers were good. Someone like Huan couldn't run and would have a difficult time hiding—never mind the helpless infants who had probably been abandoned in their cribs.

I sobbed and slapped my hands over my face. *God, why is this happening?* This wasn't what He promised me. If God was with me, then this shouldn't be happening. People shouldn't be dying.

Unless God wasn't with me anymore.

"This can't happen again!" Lanzhou shouted for at least the third time. He paced back and forth in front of the projection, his face flashing in and out of color as he walked under the sensors.

"And it won't!" Bowen insisted, trying to match his pace. "Look, I take full responsibility. This trip was my idea. I saw the laundry attendants—I should have turned around."

"Yes, you should have," Jael chided from her usual throne at the head of the table. "You're lucky you had security with you."

Everyone else is not so lucky, I thought with a whimper.

"I know, I'm sorry," Bowen pleaded, the confession directed at me. "But please, take this out on me, not her. We need her in the field." He grabbed Lanzhou's sleeve.

Lanzhou shrugged him off. "No, we don't, and I'm done having this conversation with you." He spun to face Jael. "You have to pull her from the operation and send her home."

"No!" I screeched, lurching upright. "I can't leave!"

"Philadelphia," Lanzhou sighed, the patience in his voice as thin as paper. "You can't do this anymore. You can't go out in public—and frankly, I'm not even comfortable with you staying at our house."

The statement was made with shame and regret, and he looked away as he continued. "The neighbors know we've had a houseguest for the past month. Sooner or later, someone's going to do the math, or they'll realize 'Blue Fire' doesn't always wear a brown wig."

I shivered at the thought of the Tangs' house getting burned to the ground by the police. I couldn't put Mr. Tang and his family in danger like that, not after all they'd done to help me. "I understand," I admitted. "So, I'll go somewhere else."

Lanzhou shook his head. "There isn't 'somewhere else,' Philadelphia. Not on this continent."

"I'm afraid he's right," Jael spoke up before I could object. "There are too many people in this country who know your face—and the further we expand your reach, the worse it will get. You can't be seen in public."

"Fine, take me off the PR visits, whatever," I muttered as if it didn't matter, when it definitely did. "But I can't leave Beijing."

"You have to," Lanzhou insisted. "The state is too powerful here. You need to be somewhere less populated, somewhere we haven't promoted your videos yet."

None of that mattered—why couldn't they see that? This wasn't about playing it safe; this was about doing what God told me to do. God told me I was supposed to be in Beijing, and I wasn't about to let Asia bully me out of my destiny. "But I need to be here!" I repeated. "I have to stay in China."

"I'll decide where you need to be," Jael cut in with a warning glare. "We've been over this. You can record videos remotely."

I stood up, as if adding a few inches to my height could make her understand. "This isn't about the videos!"

"Then what is it about, Philadelphia?" She groaned and leaned back in her chair, as if this whole debacle was beneath her.

I hesitated, twisting my skirt in my fingers. I hadn't told anyone about Nic's vision, not even Stanyard—probably because I knew they wouldn't believe me.

"Philadelphia," Jael threatened. "What are you not telling me?"

I took a deep breath and forced the truth out. "God told me He wanted me in Beijing."

There was a moment of utter silence. Then Jael arched her eyebrow.

"What do you mean, 'God told you'?" Bowen asked, voice laced with suspicion.

My soul cracked. Of all people, I thought Bowen would believe me. "I mean He *told* me!" I insisted, raising my voice as if that could make it sound true even to my ears. "He gave Nic a vision—"

"What about Nic?" Lanzhou interrupted.

Jael didn't give me a chance to explain. "Philadelphia, for the last time, you need to let him go."

"I can't let him go! He had a dream about me!" Even I realized how that sounded, but I pressed on. "Before we got separated, he told me God had given him a vision about me. He said he saw me in Beijing, fighting Asia."

Bowen and Lanzhou shared an uneasy glance. Lanzhou looked like he might believe me, but neither of them spoke in my defense.

"Don't you see?" I begged, reaching out with both hands. "I'm supposed to stay in China. That's the whole reason all of this happened—Red Rain, the Nolans, everything. God wants me to be here!"

"Look, I don't know what Nic saw or didn't see," Jael said in a tone that suggested she had her own opinions, "but I know you're here because I brought you here, and I can see now that was a mistake. I was wrong—you can't handle this." She stood up and strode towards the door.

I ran after her. "No, it wasn't a mistake! This is what I'm called to do!"

She didn't even look back at me. "I should have sent you to the doctor weeks ago. You're clearly not coping."

I froze, a weight dropping to my stomach. Did she really think I was sick?

Jael paused in front of the door and pointed one neon-colored fingernail at Lanzhou. "Call your physician and have them refill her prescription. She needs to sleep tonight."

The thought of being drugged filled me with dread. I couldn't lose control again, not now. "I'm not going back on medication!"

"I promise, it will make you feel better." Jael made no effort to soften her voice as she pulled out her phone and started typing.

I stared at her, my throat suddenly dry. "I just told you I heard from God," I squeaked. "Are you even listening to me?"

"I'm listening," she snapped, "and what I'm hearing is a traumatized teenager who hasn't slept in weeks and probably has undiagnosed depression." She finally spared me a glance. "Philadelphia, I know you think you had a vision, but it's just your brain trying to cope. This isn't healthy, and I'm not going to let you hurt yourself."

Tears welled up in my eyes as my friendship with Jael evaporated like smoke. She really thought I was crazy. She thought I was sick and diseased and making the whole thing up.

But I *wasn't* making it up. Nic had seen a vision that prophesied I was supposed to be in Beijing. He wouldn't lie to me—God wouldn't lie to me.

And if God wanted me to do this, then I didn't care if anyone else believed me. I would do what I had to do, even if I had to do it alone.

"Fine." I wiped my eyes as resolve dried my tears. "If that's what you think, then I'm leaving."

The room went silent, as if my words had stopped time. It took Jael several seconds to react. "What?"

"I'm leaving." I measured out each syllable to make sure I was understood. "I don't care if you don't believe me. I know what I heard, and I'm going to do what the Lord told me to do. So, if you won't help me, I'll find someone who will."

"Phil," Bowen warned, moving towards me.

Jael put up a hand to stop him. She locked eyes with me. "Is that what you really want to do? Because that sounds like insubordination."

I returned her gaze. "If you can't listen to the Lord, then I can't follow you."

She let my words hang there, forming a glass wall between us. Then she sighed. For a brief second, her cold expression wavered, and she looked genuinely upset. "Then you're not my Blue Fire."

"What?" I exclaimed.

Her voice hardened again as she returned to her phone. "I created Blue Fire. She can be replaced."

My heart restarted as a new emotion pumped through my veins. "You can't replace me!"

"I can, and I will if it will save this revolution." She swiped a command into her screen. "You're going back to Boston, and you're going off the grid for a week while I clean up this mess. Then I'll decide if you're recording any more videos."

I lost all words as my respect for her shattered. She'd become just like every other adult in my life—refusing to hear me and resorting to threats when I failed fit her mold.

She resumed dictating before I could find my voice. "Find a room for her to stay in," she ordered Bowen. "She does not leave this building until we're ready to fly out. Lock the door if you have to."

"But—" he protested.

"If I find she's set even one foot outside this factory, it's on your head," she snapped without mercy. She turned to Lanzhou. "I'm ordering some sleep medication—make sure she takes it."

"Did you just threaten to drug me and lock me in my room?" I screeched.

"You made your choice, Philadelphia." She put her back to me. "Now you can either make this easy on yourself, or you can force me to do what I must to protect my people." Then she opened the door and breezed into the hall, ending the conversation.

"But you can't—" I started, lurching forward.

Lanzhou gripped my shoulders. "Philadelphia, please."

I turned to look up at his face. He was heartbroken.

"Let me talk to Jael," Bowen insisted.

"No," Lanzhou cut him off. "You've done enough. I'll handle this. Come on, Philadelphia." He scooped my duffle and backpack off the table, then nudged me towards the door.

I was too stunned to resist. Lanzhou took advantage of my silence and gently pushed me out into the hall. I numbly let him guide me to the elevator, my feet tripping over each other as my thoughts started and stopped like an engine that was struggling to ignite.

Lanzhou led me to an abandoned office on the second floor. It was a tiny room with a tiny window and no furniture except a dusty desk.

"I'll have a cot and some dinner sent up," he said as he shoved me the rest of the way inside. He set my duffle and backpack next to the door.

I whipped around to face him. "Lanzhou, please, listen to me. You believe me, don't you? About Nic?"

He didn't answer. He stared at me, all the joy stripped from his expression. Then his eyes shifted to the keypad on the door.

I reached for the handle. "Don't, please—"

"I'm sorry," he whispered, then slammed and locked the door.

The sinister beep of the keypad sent my heart to my throat. This couldn't be happening—I *wouldn't* let it happen. I couldn't become a prisoner again, trapped behind a locked door while someone else decided my future.

I had to get out of here. I wasn't about to get drugged and thrown on a plane back to Boston. I had to get as far away from this factory as possible before Jael realized I was gone.

I spun around and scanned the room. *The window!* I ran to it and cranked the blinds open. In a stroke of luck, the office faced the back of the factory where the docks were. If I waited until nightfall, the alley would be abandoned.

Except I couldn't afford to wait. Lanzhou would return any minute with sleep medication, and he would force me to take it. I had to run *now*.

I shoved the window open, the ungreased hinges protesting. The office was two stories up, a decent drop—but there were several open dumpsters in the alley. If I could aim my fall just right…

I grabbed the sill, swung my leg up—and stopped.

What are you doing?

I wasn't sure if it was my subconscious or the Lord speaking, but He probably would have used the same tone of voice.

I jerked back from the sill as if it had burned me. I held up my hands and realized they were shaking. *Everything* was shaking. My heart was hammering and my ears were rattling as I sucked in breaths over and over without getting any air. The room pitched to one side as my vision faded in and out, like a light that was short-circuiting.

I slapped my hands to my face, but I couldn't feel them. Had I really almost just jumped out a window? What was wrong with me? I tried to answer that question, but all I found was confusion and fear and rage.

This wasn't right. None of this was right. This wasn't what God had promised—why couldn't anyone see that? Why was everything going wrong when I was doing what the Lord told me to do? Had Nic lied to me? I didn't believe that. Did he misinterpret what the vision meant? I didn't believe that either. So, what was I doing wrong? Where was God?

And why won't He answer me?

I collapsed to the floor on my knees. I'd never felt so alone in my life. I'd gone through periods of missing the Lord's voice in the chaos before, but nothing like this. He'd only spoken to me once in the past month: *"Wake My people up."* Sure, I'd preached to people at church, but that was just repeating what I already knew. I'd only received one word from the Lord for myself, and I thought I was doing what He wanted. But since then, it had been radio silence, and now everything was crumbling, and people were dead because of me, and everybody thought I was lying about Nic's vision, and absolutely nothing was happening like God said it would.

And I couldn't help but wonder if it was my fault.

Did I sin? Was this because of what happened with the General and my chip? Or was it because I almost killed Nic? Did I mess up so badly that God had chosen someone else?

I would have. I would have chosen anyone but me.

I pounded my fist into the floor and relished the shudder of pain in my arm. Maybe I *should* go home. Maybe I should give up, stop recording videos, and let someone else be Blue Fire. If God wasn't with me, then I certainly shouldn't be leading the revolution, let alone a church service.

But what would Nic say? He'd sacrificed everything—his reputation, his freedom, Mars—to get me here. What would he think if he found out I gave up and walked away? I would have given anything to talk to him, but I couldn't. I couldn't talk to Nic, I couldn't talk to my brother, I couldn't talk to my dad, and I couldn't…

I stopped when I remembered there was one person I could call. Suddenly, through the blinding hurricane of doubt and terror, I knew what I needed to do.

I dragged my backpack towards me and scraped at the zipper. I yanked my tablet out and called Stanyard.

It rang once, twice, three times. "Please pick up!" I wailed, starting to cry. I knew in my heart that if he didn't answer the first time, I'd lose my nerve.

By the grace of God, he picked up on the fifth ring.

"Hey, Phil," he mumbled groggily. His video connected, but there was nothing to see. The room was completely dark except for the backlight of his screen faintly illuminating his face. Clearly, I'd woken him up, but I didn't care.

"Stanyard," I begged, "I need you."

"Whoa, what's wrong?" The camera jerked as he struggled to detangle himself from the sheets.

"I almost jumped out a window!" I declared, then burst into tears when all the confusion and fear came rushing back.

"What?" There was a crash and a yelp, and then a lamp flicked on. He came back into frame. "You did what?"

I realized how that sounded. "No, no, not like that, I mean I almost ran away."

He tried desperately to rub the sleep from his eyes. "But why? What's going on?"

I struggled to figure out where it had all gone wrong. "They busted the group home, and we almost got caught, and a bunch of people got shot, and now Jael wants to send me back to Boston—"

"Philadelphia," Stanyard interrupted. "Slower."

I took a deep breath, even though it sounded like I swallowed water. "I visited a group home today, and someone must have given the police a tip, because they found us. I got away," I added quickly when I saw him start to react, "but they arrested several others. A couple of people got shot."

I flinched. It sounded so callous, so informative, like I was just relaying the weather. Several people *died* today—and it was because I was there.

"Phil," Stanyard breathed. I could hear the anguish in his voice, but I pushed on before he could say anything more.

"And now the government is promoting the video and making it look like I'm a murderer. Jael thinks I can't do this anymore—it's too dangerous for me to go out in public. But I *know* I'm supposed to be here."

The world shook like an earthquake when I realized I wasn't sure I believed that anymore. I repeated it again, desperate for something to make sense. "But I know that's what God wants, and I tried to tell her, but she thinks I'm insane. She really thinks I'm sick, Stanyard. She threatened to put me on medication."

I searched Stanyard's eyes, begging him to believe me. Surely, someone had to agree that this wasn't right.

He did. His eyes narrowed. "Where are you now?"

"At the factory. Lanzhou locked me in an office. Jael wants to send me back to Boston, but I know this isn't right. I wanted to run away, but I know that's not right either, and I just…" My voice shattered as my emotions came out in a garbled torrent. "I'm scared and confused and I don't want to take any pills, but she's not listening to me and I don't know what to do… so I called you."

I broke off in a sob, that last statement putting a period on my pathetic existence.

Jael was right. I couldn't handle this.

Stanyard was silent for a long moment, long enough that I began to worry I'd scared him off. I swallowed and forced myself to look down at the screen.

He was smiling, the gesture completely dissonant from the cold darkness in my heart.

"What?" I prodded.

"Did you hear what you just said? You called me *before* you made a decision." The joy was so thick in his voice that he sounded like he was two steps away from crying himself. "I'm so proud of you, Phil."

A tiny sliver of warmth crawled into my soul when I realized he wasn't the only one. I felt the shift in the Spirit and tried to grasp the feeling before it slipped away.

Please don't go. I need You.

Stanyard sat cross-legged on his bed and held the camera out in front of him. "Now, talk to me. Why do you think you shouldn't come back to Boston?"

I struggled to gather the thoughts that were scattered on the floor of my mind like pieces of shredded paper.

"Is it because of Nic?" Stanyard prompted when I didn't speak for a minute.

The Holy Spirit gave me the answer to that question. "No," I admitted to myself and the Lord. "At least… not for the reason everyone thinks."

Stanyard waited.

I flinched. "This is going to sound crazy, but... you have to believe me. Please."

"Phil," he said, his gentle voice reaching across the airwaves like a hug, "I'll always believe you. I can't promise that I'll always agree with your decisions, but I'll always believe you."

I stared into his eyes as mine welled up again.

"Do you trust me, Phil?"

"Okay." I took a long breath and waited until my heart stopped thrumming in my ears before speaking again. Then I walked him through everything as best I could—about Nic's vision, my conversation with Tower, the command the Lord had given me. I laid it all out in the open—for Stanyard and myself—and explained why I knew in my heart of hearts that I was supposed to be in Beijing.

"I know that sounds insane, but..." I stopped when I realized there was no second half to that sentence. I sighed and braced myself for his reaction.

He let his breath out through his nose. "I'll admit, this completely reframes the way I think about Nic." The statement was too genuine to be sarcastic. "But, coming from you, it doesn't really surprise me. To be honest, I suspected it had to be something like that."

I scrunched my brow. "What do you mean?" An open vision was the last thing I would have suspected.

"Phil, don't take this the wrong way, but..." Stanyard almost smiled as he confessed, "You're kind of emotional. It's really not that hard to convince you to change your mind, especially if there's hurting people involved."

I flushed when I realized he was right.

He put up his hand. "Don't overthink it. All I'm saying is, the only time you dig in your heels is when you believe you're doing what's right. The fact that you've been so adamant about staying in Beijing when it's really dangerous tells me that God's involved somewhere."

"Then you believe me," I stated, relief finally putting the breath back in my lungs.

"Of course," he said without hesitation. "I absolutely believe God called you to be Blue Fire. I've never doubted that."

He paused, and I filled in the blanks. "But...?"

"But I think you're going about this the wrong way. Just because God said you're supposed to be in Beijing doesn't mean you're supposed to be there *right now*. And what if you've already accomplished what He wanted you to do? He could have..."

Stanyard trailed off, as if he realized he was using too many words. He glanced away and drummed his fingers on his knee. I held my tongue, even though every nerve in my body wanted to argue.

Stanyard finally condensed his thoughts and turned back to the camera. "Remember Abraham and Issac?"

"Yeah?"

"God told him he was going to have a son—but it didn't happen for, like, twenty-five years."

I stiffened. For the first time in the last hour, my head stopped ringing as Stanyard's words reset my reality.

"And what about Joseph? God told him he was going to rule the world, but then he got sold into slavery and sentenced to jail for something he didn't do. And David—he could have killed Saul in that cave."

I knew exactly what passage he was talking about. I grabbed my backpack and pulled out my Bible. I flipped through the pages until I found what I was looking for:

"The men said, 'This is the day the Lord spoke of when he said to you, "I will give your enemy into your hands for you to deal with as you wish."' Then David crept up unnoticed and cut off a corner of Saul's robe.

"Afterward, David was conscience-stricken for having cut off a corner of his robe. He said to his men, 'The Lord forbid that I should do such a thing to my master, the Lord's anointed, or lay my hand on him; for he is the anointed of the Lord.' With these words David sharply rebuked his men and did not allow them to attack Saul."

"David could have made himself king," Stanyard spoke into the silence as the Scripture sank its teeth into my soul. "But he didn't, because he knew God would fulfill His promise in His time."

I closed my eyes.

"Phil, you said yourself, you didn't create Blue Fire. Jael did."

I nodded as several tears slid down my face.

"If you didn't create her, then you don't have to protect her. You don't have to make this happen. If God wants you to do something in China, then He'll open the door. Maybe it's today, maybe it's next week. Maybe it's not for a few years. I don't know—and you don't either."

And that's okay, the Holy Spirit echoed him.

I opened my eyes. I knew what I had to do.

"I gotta go," I announced.

"Wait," Stanyard called. "Look, take it from someone who's done this before: It will be scary. You're going to feel like you're breaking apart and losing pieces of yourself. But I promise—you're not losing anything you want to keep."

I focused on the screen. He was smiling softly, and I found myself returning the gesture. "I'll text in half an hour," I promised, and hung up.

Tossing the tablet aside, I jumped up and closed the window and the blinds, then turned off the lights. This was between me and the Lord.

I returned to the floor and pulled my knees to my chest. I rocked in silence for a minute, almost wishing the Holy Spirit would initiate. But I knew I had to be the one to move.

"God, I'm sorry," I started—then stopped again. How was I supposed to do this?

Just tell Him the truth, I coached myself.

I closed my eyes again and rocked harder. "God, I'm sorry. I don't want to do this anymore—I mean, I don't want to do this by myself anymore. I'm tired of being alone and confused and trying to figure it out. I want to hear You again."

I shivered as that feeling of being lost at sea swept over me. "I miss You," I whispered. "I miss You, and I miss Nic, and I feel like no one else understands. I'm scared, and I don't understand why this is happening. You brought me to Beijing, but now Nic is gone and people are dying and I don't... I don't know what to do. I don't know where I went wrong."

There it was—that sharp, icy pain in my soul. That deep-rooted fear that this was all my fault, that I'd sinned and ruined my future, that God had left me and was never coming back. And underneath it all was the maddening desperation that if I just tried a little harder, held on a little tighter, I could fix this. I could prove myself. I could avoid all this pain and darkness and loneliness if I just worked harder and behaved better.

I lay down flat on the floor, but the world continued to shake. Stanyard was right—I was breaking apart. I felt like a cracked porcelain doll; if I didn't hold myself together, I would shatter into a million unrecoverable pieces. There was darkness everywhere—inside, outside, blurring my vision—like a wave capsizing a boat. If I fell in, I would drown.

I wept. I had no idea what else to do. I was trembling so hard I couldn't feel my face or my hands, and I had no idea if it was the Holy Spirit or terror that was rolling over me like a windstorm. The room seemed both too quiet and too loud at the same time. I couldn't breathe, I couldn't swallow, and I knew, no matter what, that I wasn't getting up off this floor alive.

You have to let go.

I couldn't stand it any longer. "I give up, God," I hacked, the words barely making it past the anxiety in my throat. "I surrender."

Nothing changed. The world was still dark, and the fear still screamed in my ear. Everything I knew I needed was hanging just out of reach—locked on the other side of that glass coffin I'd been trapped in for so many weeks.

I jerked upright and screamed into the empty room. "I give up!" I shouted again, desperate for whoever was on the outside of the box to hear me. "I don't have to be Blue Fire, I don't have to stay in Beijing, and I don't have to lead the revolution. If You want me to go back to Boston, I will. If You don't want me to record any more videos, I won't. If I never do anything important in my life ever again, then fine! Do what You want to do, God. I just need *You* back!"

The glass shattered. Like a breaking dam, all the emotions that had been trapped inside of me spilled onto the floor. Suddenly, I could feel myself again—I could feel *Him* again. There was peace and uncertainty and regret and forgiveness all at once, and I accepted it all. I went limp and let it wash over me, soaking up the weight of His presence until He was the only thing I was breathing.

Eventually—I had no idea how much time had passed—the waves of emotion subsided, as if the storm had blown over. I felt almost empty, but not in a frightening way. It was as if I had room to breathe again.

And into that newly created silence, the Spirit spoke.

I love you.

"I love You, too," I whispered back.

My tablet pinged. I pushed myself up and looked at the screen; it was Stanyard.

YOU OKAY?

I glanced at the clock and realized it had been a lot longer than a half hour. I quickly opened the device and texted back.

YEAH, SORRY

AND?

That one word was an invitation. And this time, I took it.

I'M COMING HOME

21: NIC

"I have to admit, I'm very disappointed, Q."

"What part of 'your profit margin has increased by 26.52%' is disappointing?"

I squinted at the graph displayed on the projector and tried to figure out what part hadn't made it past translation. Vance, Ryan, and I were gathered in Warden Ivanova's office to review production reports. It hadn't even been two weeks, and I'd already won the bet. The factory was operating at an impressive 92% efficiency. Profits had doubled, and that didn't even account for all the money they were saving on conserved resources. If the higher ups didn't recognize her achievement, the warden could just creatively "allocate" some of the surplus funds and give herself a raise.

She, however, did not seem to recognize the significance of this achievement. *Maybe I shouldn't have used a pie chart.*

She cackled. "I was really looking forward to feeding you to the lions if you lost."

"You can't win every round," I intoned.

She stood up and offered me her hand. "Then remind me to never bet against you again. Good job, Q."

Ryan whooped and jumped three feet off the ground so he could slap me on the back. Vance clapped politely and cracked something close to a smile.

I deferred the praise with a small bow. "However, if you want this to last, there's one more change you need to make."

"What's that?" she asked.

I shoved Ryan forward. "You need to make him your floor supervisor."

"Hold up! What are you volunteering me for?" Ryan struggled to get away, but I held him by the collar.

The warden sneered down her nose at him. "This guy? He can't even see over the railing."

"Then get him a stepstool. Look, I can engineer your assembly line to death, but it will fail without productive workers. If you want your prisoners to be compliant *and* happy, you need to put Ryan in charge."

I looked down at him as I revealed what the Lord had shown me, piece by piece, over the past few nights. "This guy is so good with people that he organized the most successful demonstration in a decade—and he wasn't even on the same continent."

Ryan stopped squirming. "Huh, never thought about it that way."

"Fair enough," Warden Ivanova said with a careless shrug. "Anything else I should do?"

"Yeah. You need him to do your books." I grabbed Vance's sleeve and tried to pull him forward, then gave up when I realized it would be like dragging a boulder.

Warden Ivanova frowned. "I've already got an accountant."

"Not a good one," I argued. "If you want to make sure all these increased profits are reinvested properly—and have some left over for yourself—then you need a wizard with numbers. Besides, I heard he's really good at tax fraud, and that's something you're going to need if you don't want the feds snooping into your sudden productivity boom." I punched Vance's muscular shoulder and immediately regretted it.

He folded his arms. "I told you, what I did is not considered fraud in most jurisdictions..."

I glared up at him. "Don't help me."

"Well, I can't believe I'm saying this, but I trust your judgment, Q." Warden Ivanova turned and barked at the guards standing by the door. "Get these men an office and anything else they need. I want this implemented tonight."

The guards saluted and turned to go. Ryan scampered after them, mouthing something about *"We'll talk at dinner."*

Vance followed at his own pace. When he got to the door, he stopped, glanced over his shoulder at me, and winked.

I smiled back.

"Well, seems you worked yourself out of a job, Q."

I turned to the warden. She leaned against her desk. "You've completely turned this factory around *and* given me a new management team. I don't suppose I need you anymore."

"No, not really," I admitted. "So, can I go home?"

She smirked. "Nice try. I have another job for you."

She gestured for me to follow. We walked to the elevator and descended to one of the subbasements—one of the few floors of the factory I hadn't been on. The warden pressed the button to open the doors, then stepped back to let me see.

The entire floor was a giant open lab. A glittering array of workstations and fabricators ran the perimeter of the room, and in the center was a massive testing chamber manned by two robotic arms. The space thrummed with activity as half a dozen scientists bustled around the plexiglass cube, murmuring and taking notes.

I gaped. "What else do you have hiding in your basement?"

She walked up beside me. "We don't just produce the products here—we develop them. And these Einsteins are in desperate need of leadership."

I glanced at her. She smiled and gestured broadly at the lab. "Welcome to management. I figure this is a more *profitable* use of your three PhDs."

I managed to mumble an affirmative as the Voice invaded my consciousness.

I told you I would give you this factory.

"Oh, you'll need a different uniform." Warden Ivanova walked over to a supply cabinet and opened it. She yanked a lab coat off its hanger and tossed it at me.

I caught it. "But I look so good in orange."

"You don't." She strode back to the elevator. "Make yourself comfortable. Work starts at 0900 tomorrow, Q—or should I say, Dr. Nic?"

I looked up just in time to catch her wink before the elevator doors closed.

I fingered the starched cotton as I surveyed the lab again. All the familiar sounds and smells enveloped me and put me right at home: the sterile scent of acetone and latex, the clatter of flasks on a metal table, the squeak of oxfords on the linoleum floor. The facility was a lot smaller than my station on Mars, but it was state of the art and beautiful nonetheless.

And now it was mine.

"Thank you," I said aloud.

He smiled. *Well done.*

The arrival of the elevator interrupted our bonding moment. I turned to see a breathless guard approach.

"I'm sorry, Q, I mean, Dr. Von Niewen—"

"Just Nic is fine. What's wrong?"

"Someone's here to see you."

I stared at him for a solid ten seconds before gathering my wits and following him back to the elevator. Who would be coming to visit me?

I was in such a good mood that I flirted with irrationality. *Could it be her? Did the underground find me?*

Disappointment didn't even begin to describe my reaction when I opened the visiting room door and saw Asia standing there.

"You seem surprised to see me," she cooed after we'd finished gawking at each other.

"I was just hoping it was… well, literally anyone but you."

She flicked her finger. "Come here."

"That's a nope." I pulled back into the hall and prepared to slam the door.

"It's about Philadelphia," she called, barely raising her voice.

I hesitated.

"That's what I thought. I'll ask you again: Come here."

I stepped into the room and closed the door to prevent eavesdroppers, then folded my arms and leaned against the wall.

She rolled her eyes. "How would you like a full pardon, doctor?"

I snorted. "At what price? If it involves kissing you, then no thank you. I'll take my chances in here."

She shook her head, her deathly gorgeous smile returning. "I thought we discussed this: I'm over you. All I ask is that you tell me where Philadelphia is staying, and you'll both be pardoned."

"You still haven't found her?" I guffawed. I was so elated that I doubled over and laughed maniacally. "I was already having a great day, but that's just icing on the cake. It was so nice of you to fly all the way out here to tell me the good news."

There was a pause before she retaliated, which told me all I needed to know. "I almost caught her," she growled.

"'Almost' doesn't win wars, sweetheart. Just admit it: You were bested by a homeschooled teenager. Join the club. We'll get t-shirts made."

She took a minute to collect her evil serenity before continuing. "Maybe I haven't set the stage properly. I had that building surrounded. I could have burned it down on top of her."

I wasn't fond of that mental image, but I kept a straight face. "And you didn't because...?"

"Her security shot first." Asia shrugged, as if the failure didn't bother her—and I genuinely believed that it didn't. "The rest of the people in that building were not so lucky."

I swallowed my next comeback.

Confident she'd regained control of the conversation, Asia took a menacing step forward. "They won't be able to hide her forever. Everyone knows she's in Beijing, and the entire province is in an uproar."

I'd always known that was a risk; that was why I hadn't wanted us to stay in China in the first place. But I knew Phil had a calling—and I knew Who had called her. For the first time in a long time, Asia was not in control.

She wrinkled her nose, as if my silence was disappointing. "I *will* find her," she announced, raising her voice to compensate for my lack of theatrics. "And if the police catch her first, they will burn her at the stake. Do you really want to see her go through that? The trial, the humiliation?"

"What do you want, Asia?" I barked. "Get to the point before you suck all the oxygen out of the room."

She tipped her chin back. "I'm here to make a deal. Tell me where she is, and I'll make this all go away. You know I don't want to hurt her. I'll get her to safety, and all her friends can go free."

Terrifyingly, I knew she was telling the truth. She would do as she promised—and that was precisely why I couldn't agree.

"If the government finds her, they will kill her. But *you* can still save her, Nic." Asia stretched her hand towards me, her fingernails sharpened to a point like knives. "Let me help you save her. If you care about her—"

I pushed away from the wall. "You know what, Asia? You're right."

She stopped.

I threw up my hands in surrender. "You have me completely figured out. I do care about Phil. I care about her more than anyone I've ever cared about before—including you."

She *tched*, but the sound fell short.

"But do you know what that means?"

I closed the gap between us. She straightened and stared me down. I leaned over until my face was inches from hers, enunciating each syllable slowly as I drew my line in the sand.

"I won't let you have her. I'll serve every single minute of my seventeen life sentences before I let you touch her. So, either shoot me now or get back in your helicopter and fly away, because I'd rather die than tell you where she is."

There was a pause as she contemplated me. Then she huffed and stepped aside. "Funny, that's what the rebels I tortured earlier today said."

"What?"

She reached into the pocket of her suitcoat and pulled out her phone. "I've been playing nice so far, but I've got a deadline approaching, so we're going to speed this up." She tapped the screen. "As of today, the price on her life is doubled. Anyone who even calls in a tip will be handsomely rewarded. On the contrary, anyone who is suspected of harboring her will be considered an enemy of the state."

She looked up and met my eyes one last time. "Mark my words: I will turn this entire city against her."

"That will work great," I snapped, filtering out my emotions, "until she leaves the country."

Asia blinked, as if she hadn't considered that before. Then, slowly, her lips parted in a sneer. I saw a flash of her white teeth as she ran her tongue over them. "What a brilliant idea, doctor." She moved to walk past me.

"Wait, what do you mean? Asia!"

I reached for her arm—and my hand went straight through. The hologram glitched as my fingers disturbed the particles.

She cackled. "I mean, you didn't think I'd really come and see you, did you? This place is disgusting."

She stepped through me, her image briefly phasing in and out of existence. "Enjoy your retirement, doctor. But while you're counting off your five hundred and ten years of incarceration, remember this." She paused and glanced over her shoulder. "You could have prevented what's about to happen."

And then she walked out of frame and disappeared.

22: PHILADELPHIA

The next morning found me standing alone outside the conference room.

The sun had just peaked above the skyline and was warming the shadowy hall with yellow light. I'd spoken to Lanzhou the night before and asked him to arrange a meeting with Jael. Somewhat to my surprise, she'd consented to meet with me early, before the others arrived. The off-duty factory was eerily quiet, with the only sound being the distant beep of a truck as it backed up to the delivery dock.

I fidgeted with the strap of my bag. I had used the black duffle Narissa sent as a suitcase and organized my tiny stash of worldly belongings into it. I was sure I'd have a chance to go by the Tangs' house and pick up the rest of my clothes—and my cat—but I wanted to be ready when I met with Jael.

Partially because if I wasn't packed to leave, I knew there was a risk I would change my mind.

I closed my eyes and fought back a wave of uncertainty. Everything still felt dark and scary and watery, like I'd cut the anchor and was drifting listlessly out to sea. Surrendering to the Lord didn't answer all my questions; if anything, I had *more* questions as my vision of my future broke apart like a wrecked lifeboat.

But despite the anxiety that still squeezed my soul, there was one emotion I wasn't feeling anymore: anger. I could tell in my jaw and down my back; I wasn't tense. And that gentle sense of quiet spoke louder than all the doubts and promised me I was doing the right thing.

Not my will, I preached to myself, then pressed the doorbell on the conference room.

Jael answered immediately. "Come in, Philadelphia."

I swallowed my nerves and opened the door.

She was alone, as I'd requested. She was in her usual place at the head of the table, one leg crossed over the other as she worked on a laptop. The projector behind her was playing the morning news, the sound muted.

Suddenly, the conference table seemed a mile long, like the final walk on death row. I hesitated, long enough that the door began to shut again. I quickly caught it with my arm and forced myself to put one foot in front of the other.

Jael did not look up until I arrived in front of her. "Yes?" she prompted, the word devoid of opinion.

I tossed my duffle and my backpack on the table. "I'm going back to Boston."

She glanced at my bags. "You don't have a choice."

"I always have a choice," I returned. "But I'm choosing to obey you."

She shifted her eyes back to my face. "Why?"

"Because you're in charge," I said simply, and that was that.

She arched a plucked eyebrow. "Did you call me in here at the crack of dawn just to tell me something I already knew?"

"No." I stood up straight. "I called you in because I wanted to apologize."

She leaned back in her seat and waited.

"I want to apologize for my behavior yesterday. What I said was very insensitive, and it was immature of me to threaten to run away. I disrespected you in front of the others, and I'm sorry."

If she was impressed by this confession, she didn't show it. I took a deep breath and pressed on. "I hope I can still be part of the operation. I want to stream from Boston, if you'll let me."

"And what if I say no?" she challenged.

I tried to read her tone for a cue but couldn't find one. I resisted the urge to cry as I gave up my last piece of control. "Then I understand. If you tell me I'm done, I'm done. You have my word that I will not go behind your back, and I will not try to undermine you. I trust your judgment, so whatever you tell me to do, I'll do it."

She let my words hang there for a moment. "Is that all?"

"Yes, ma'am." I folded my hands and awaited my sentence.

"Then that's all I needed to hear." The light came back into her eyes as she smiled and set her laptop aside.

Every muscle in my body relaxed as forgiveness washed over me. I let out the breath I'd been unintentionally holding.

Jael chuckled and stood up. "At ease, soldier." And then she did the unthinkable: She opened her arms for a hug.

I hesitated, but only for a second. I grasped her and soaked up the physical affection I had been needing for so many weeks.

She rubbed my shoulders. "You'll always be my Blue Fire," she whispered in my ear.

And Mine, I felt the Holy Spirit say. I didn't bother to blink away the tears.

She gave me another pat and let go. I pulled back—just in time to see myself come on TV.

It was a clip from yesterday's raid. The footage was grainy, pulled from the security camera on the building across the street and enlarged. Some helpful editor had drawn a yellow circle around my blurry face as I slipped away down the alley and disappeared.

The video paused, and the anchorwoman took over. She read from her script as Mandarin characters flashed across the screen. "What does it say?" I asked Jael.

She frowned and stroked her fingers across a tablet lying on the conference table. The sound came on, but I couldn't understand any of the foreign language. Jael hit another button, and a rote, slightly inhuman voice replaced the anchorwoman's and began to speak in English.

"In response to the continued violence of this terrorist group, United leadership has increased the reward for any information regarding the whereabouts of Philadelphia Smyrna." The AI voice lagged a few seconds behind the anchorwoman's lip movements as it translated. "Beijing officials are asking for help identifying several of Smyrna's associates who were photographed at last night's riot."

The security footage zoomed out to reveal several other figures fleeing down the fire escape, their faces highlighted in an ethereal white. My heart caught in my throat when I recognized one of them as Bowen. Thankfully, he was facing away from the camera, so only his side profile was caught on tape. *Had he turned around...*

I closed my eyes and prayed, hard.

"Investigators have already used face-recognition and location services to detain several of the terrorists," the anchorwoman droned, as if this information were about as interesting as a traffic report. "Following positive confessions regarding their involvement with so-called 'Operation Blue Fire,' the terrorists have been convicted and their executions scheduled for this afternoon."

My eyes flew open. "What?"

She needn't have repeated herself. The screen flashed to a livestream of a sports stadium. Civilians were trickling in, shaded with irreverently colored umbrellas as they claimed the best seats. I could tell by the row of armed soldiers lining the perimeter of the field that they were not setting up for a game.

The ugly truth sank into me like fangs. That was why some of my guards hadn't made it back; they'd been captured and sentenced to death, along with all the other innocent nurses and sick residents who hadn't made it out of the building. The government was going to slaughter them all.

A sound I don't remember summoning ripped out of me. *They can't do this!* But I knew they would; the Chinese government had been executing people like cattle for a century.

The sentencing of a few unassimilated criminals was hardly worth reporting.

Except they were associated with me.

I whipped to face Jael. "Please, is there anything we can do? I know you've gotten people off death row before."

She squinted at the projector, jaw set like a rock. Before she could answer, Asia appeared on the screen.

Her cruel face filled the monitor as she radioed in. "It is with a heavy heart that I signed off on these executions this morning," she said, the AI translating from Mandarin. "These 'rebels' were regular citizens until Smyrna poisoned them with a false promise of wealth and power."

They flashed up a clip from one of my recent videos—the one where a troop of soldiers saluted me, their guns pointed towards the sky. The clip that made me look like a deadly insurrectionist.

I buckled over and gripped my chest. *Oh God, what have I done?* That wasn't who Blue Fire was at all. But Asia would twist and corrupt and edit my photos until the entire world thought of me as a dictator—and thanks to my recent rallies, I had given her plenty of material.

The screen split between the anchorwoman and Asia as the broadcast returned to the studio. "Clearly, this 'operation' has become a front for glorified gang violence," the anchorwoman prompted.

Asia bobbed her head. "Indeed. And I fear for our young people. The rebels' propaganda is blatantly targeting our most vulnerable..."

Jael spoke over her. "You're going on air."

I stumbled back from the projection. "What?"

She whipped around and opened her laptop. "I'm patching you in. I can hijack this broadcast with Data's program."

"But why?" I gasped, then quickly changed the question. "What do you want me to say?"

"Just keep Asia talking." Jael's nails clacked rapidly on the keys like gunfire. "You're buying me time. As long as you're on air, her people will be scrambling to figure out where you're broadcasting from. If I can send them on a rabbit trail for even an hour, that gives me a window to stop these executions."

I reacted and grabbed my duffle. I popped my blue contacts out and threw them on the table, then slid the wig on and stuffed my blonde hair underneath. It was sloppy, but it would have to do. I stripped my jacket, exposing my thunderbird tattoo, and turned to Jael.

She spun the laptop around to face me. "She will be able to see you."

I sank into the chair in front of the computer, my knees suddenly wobbly. *Oh God, help me! Give me the words!*

Jael brushed my shoulder. "I'll help you. Just follow my lead." She stepped back and grabbed the tablet, muting the projection. "You're on in three, two…"

Before she even got to "one," the image on the newscast glitched, and I was there. My crackly stream replaced the anchorwoman's, so it looked like Asia and I were sitting side by side.

Jael gestured frantically at her lips. I swallowed my trepidation and spoke loudly to cover my own fears. "This is Blue Fire. Can you hear me?"

Apparently, they could. There was a sharp beep, and my stream flickered, replaced with the irritated words "technical difficulties." I looked to Jael in a panic. Had they finally patched Data's backdoor?

"Wait!" Asia shouted in English, lunging forward. "Let her through."

There was a pause, and then my stream faded in again. The camera autofocused until I was coming through clearly.

"That's better." Asia settled back in her chair. "Philadelphia, what a surprise. I see you've finally decided to show your face."

Jael made a rolling motion, so I blurted the first thing that came to mind. "You must not have social media," I snarked, trying to sound bored like Nic, "because I show my face all the time. So much so that I heard your algorithm has a censorship filter for it."

I glanced at Jael for approval. She winked encouragingly and continued to swipe commands into her tablet.

Asia snorted. "How unbecoming. Philadelphia, what *are* you doing?"

Jael took up station on the other side of the table and faced her tablet towards me. On the screen she'd typed in large letters: *"Turn the question back on her."*

"What are *you* doing, Asia?" I returned, mimicking her tone. "I know you're trying to bait me with all these theatrics. These trials and executions—is that what this has come to?"

Asia shook her head. "You can't blame me for your problems, child. You brought this on yourself. That blood is on your hands."

Jael held up another prompt: *"Remind them who the real enemy is."*

"No, it's on yours." I sat up straight as righteous anger filled me with resolve. "That wasn't a 'rebel hideout' you busted yesterday—it was a *hospital*. There were helpless *babies* in that apartment. What did you do with those children, Asia?"

She ignored the last question. "You call that a hospital? Those children were living in squalid conditions and being denied medical care. And when I send in social workers to try to rescue them, you open fire."

My palms began to sweat. "They were just trying to protect me. *Your* government is the one who came in and shot a dozen unarmed people—and now they're going to execute the rest of them."

The words hitched in my throat as I remembered what was at stake. Jael smiled.

Asia held up her hand, as if forestalling someone off-screen. "That sounds like exactly the kind of thing a divisive terrorist would say. You've become just like the rest of them—using race and religion to cover up your thirst for power. I know the real you, Philadelphia, and all you want is war."

"No, I don't," I insisted. "*You* do."

Asia hesitated for a second, long enough for Jael to swipe to the next screen: *"Tell her you're leaving town."*

I met her eyes, searching for confirmation. She nodded.

I focused back on the camera. "But I won't give it to you. If this is the game you want, then I'm not going to play. I'm leaving town, and you won't be able to find me. I'll be gone by nightfall."

The silence dragged on, so long that I wondered if she hadn't heard me. But then, slowly, she grinned.

"Oh, Philadelphia," she crooned, "don't you know it's too late to go home?"

My heart froze.

She turned and gestured at someone off-camera. "Roll the clip."

The newscast rearranged. Our streams were shoved to the corner to make room for a full screen feed of a downtown street. A dozen wailing police cars circled an old stone office building as a regiment of soldiers swarmed the sidewalk. A commander supervised the chaos, barking orders into a megaphone.

At first, I couldn't see any landmarks, but the slant of the light suggested the sun was setting, putting the scene on the opposite side of the world. And then I caught sight of a street sign: The office was on the corner of Bolyston and Washington. I knew that intersection; it was in downtown Boston.

I choked when I realized what was about to happen. *No!*

Asia confirmed my fears. "I'm very pleased to report that, thanks to an anonymous tip, we've located Smyrna's American headquarters," she announced.

"Who told you?" I screeched.

She ignored me. "This building was the main hub of operations for 'Blue Fire,'" she explained, voice clearly not directed at me anymore. "Police have recovered multiple servers of valuable information, and several of her co-conspirators have been detained."

As if on cue, the front door of the building banged open, and a pair of guards hauled someone onto the sidewalk.

"Stanyard!" I screamed, forgetting I was on air.

I barely caught a glimpse as they shoved him, cuffed and struggling, into the back of a van. Right behind him, two more guards were arresting Lev. His tennis shoes scraped on the concrete as they literally dragged him by his collar. I saw a distinct smear of blood on his pale cheek before they threw him into the van.

I scrambled for my backpack, not caring that I was no longer in frame. *Oh God, no no no.* I snatched my tablet and dialed Stanyard. *This can't be happening, this can't be happening, this can't be happening.*

It rang out.

Jael threw her tablet on the table. She whipped around and began whispering harshly into her phone.

I numbly sank back into the chair. I hyperventilated, the air scraping my throat like gravel, as my thoughts started and stopped, started and stopped. *He's dead. Stanyard is dead, Lev is dead, they're all going to die!*

"I have an announcement for all United citizens." Asia raised her voice to be heard over the shouting as the footage continued to roll. "As of today, the reward for information regarding the whereabouts of Philadelphia Smyrna has doubled."

The guards dragged someone else out of the building: my uncle. Two soldiers held him down while they took a thumbprint scan and cuffed his hands behind his back.

The soldier frowned at his tablet and handed it to their commander. The commander took one look and hurled the device on the sidewalk. He lunged at Tower, shoving his shoulders and cussing him out.

That's when I remembered my uncle was military. That meant he was worse than a rebel; he was a traitor.

"All citizens are authorized to detain her and any of her associates by any means necessary." Asia couldn't keep the smile off her face as she narrated. "On the other hand, be advised that associating with or harboring Smyrna will be considered an act of terrorism."

The commander spit in Tower's face, then took a step back. The other soldiers forced my uncle to his knees on the sidewalk.

I saw the commander reach for his holster and knew what was coming a second before it happened.

"Stop, Asia, please!" I shrieked. "Don't do this!"

She spoke as if she didn't hear me. "And the punishment for terrorism…"

I screamed, but the explosion from the commander's gun drowned me out.

"…is death."

Someone yelled in the background, and then the footage went oddly silent. The soldiers gracelessly dropped Tower's body on the curb. The camera continued to roll, the gruesome scene letting the entire world know my uncle was dead.

And it was all because of me.

Tears streamed down my face. I was breathing so hard you could hear it on the TV as I gripped the table and struggled not to black out. *God, what is happening?*

Asia's cackle jerked me back to the cruel present. "I only have one thing to say to you, Philadelphia."

I instinctively turned to face her.

She held me in her wicked glare. "Checkmate," she sneered, and then the screen went dark.

TO BE CONTINUED…

WANT EXCLUSIVE BONUS SCENES?

Become a Patron and get access to **exclusive bonus scenes** for this book! This bonus content is not available anywhere else, and I post a new scene every month. Plus, you can get digital ARCs, signed paperbacks, collector's edition hardbacks, and merch, or read my WIP as I write it!

Become a Patron at:
patreon.com/rachelnewhouse

Or sign up for my newsletter and be the first to hear about new releases—plus get sneak peeks of upcoming books, cover art, and more!

Sign up at:
rachelnewhouse.com/subscribe

DID YOU LOVE THIS BOOK?

Please consider leaving a review on Amazon or Goodreads! It's one of the most important things you can do to support an indie author. Thank you!

HI FROM RACHEL

Rachel Newhouse is an author, wife, secretary, and Sunday school teacher from Kansas City, Missouri. Her obsessions are sci-fi, dystopian, and kid lit. When she's not writing, she's cooking Asian food, growing chilis that are too spicy to eat, and watching wildly age-inappropriate shows like *My Little Pony* and *Gravity Falls* with her husband, Joe. She also really likes glitter. You've been warned.

Connect with Rachel:
bio.site/rachelnewhouse

www.ingramcontent.com/pod-product-compliance
Lightning Source LLC
Chambersburg PA
CBHW070503200726
48293CB00007B/2350